MW01632502

homerville

by
Ken Bradbury

The Consortium Publishing
PO Box 998
Jacksonville IL 62651

homerville is written by Ken Bradbury of Arenzville, Illinois. Ken writes a weekly syndicated newspaper column under the name of Freida Marie Crump, news correspondent from Coonridge, Illinois. Freida (Ken) has three previous books: *Coonridge Digest, Around the World With Freida Marie Crump,* and *Coonridge Devotions.*

The Consortium Publishing Company
(A Division of Creative Ideas, Inc.)
PO Box 1535
Jacksonville, IL 62651-1535
888-456-7235
Fax: 217-243-7628
consortm@aol.com
www.creativeideas.com

Editor: Robert L. Crowe
Library of Congress Control Number: 2005929561
ISBN Number: 0-9748830-1-8
Printed by Cenveo Press, Jacksonville, IL
1 2 3 4 5 6 7 8 9 10

FOREWARD

In my senior year of high school, I was fortunate enough to make it to the state championship in public speaking. The extempore speakers were narrowed down to our final six, and I stood before the judge to give my six-minute speech then walked back to his desk for comments. The old man raised a pair of extremely bushy eyebrows and said, "You're from Pike County, aren't you?"

I was astounded. It was strictly forbidden for a judge to know anything about the contestant other than the speaker's name. And besides that, how did he know? I was a farm boy but my shoes were shined as nicely as my opponents' from the Chicago suburbs. I was wearing my dad's best tie and probably reeked of Old Spice after shave but how could that possibly label my place of origin?

I said, "Yes. Yes, sir, I am."

"Thought so," he mused. "It's your speech pattern. It sure sounds like Pike."

I learned later that the old professor had spent his lifetime studying the dialects of Illinois, so his linguistic sleuthing was perhaps not all that earth shaking.

Then I went to college and sat around the dormitory listening to my classmates tell of their high school classes of 800 students, their advanced classes in Greek Literature and Neo-classic Architecture, and I can remember wondering whether a boy from Perry, Illinois, had enough life experiences to make it in such a wide-flung world.

I come from a family of storytellers who live in a region where the oral tradition of local history is still very much a part of the everyday conversation. If you buy a house in Pike County we can not only tell you who has lived there for the past hundred years but we know a thing or two about what they did, thought, and felt. In Central Illinois, this is not regarded as being nosey, simply, well … concerned.

Every story in this collection has its roots in fact. The leaves and stems I may have embroidered a bit to fill a gap or protect a still living descendent. And it is to the remarkable residents of that pregnant hump on the west side of Illinois that I give my thanks.

Ken Bradbury, August 2005

Darby's Throne

Darby's left foot would catch on each of the wooden steps as he made his nightly crawl up to his throne. That's what Dad called it … Darby's Throne.

Darby Sitton lived just east of us on the west edge of town. His rambling two-story frame house was a jumble of repairs, patches, and just plain poor fixing. Everything in Darby's life was done on the cheap. If a door fell off, he nailed it shut and used another. His broken windows proclaimed "SEARS" as packing crates were duct-taped across the cracks. Darby Sitton was the richest man in town and he had not earned his little fortune by spending foolishly on window glass.

Even Darby's Throne was a study in time saving. The town had waited until the early 1970's to purchase its own sewer system, so the more affluent households were flush with septic tanks while the older folks still relied on the outdoor privy. But privy digging takes work and Darby couldn't be bothered. Instead of digging a pit then constructing an outdoor john, Darby built a platform some twelve feet in the air, cut a hole in the caning of an abandoned kitchen chair, and placed it over a similar hole on the platform.

Each night, while there was still light enough for him and the entire world to see, Darby would climb the dozen steps to his throne and sit there like the king of Homerville, surveying his realm as his bowels emptied below him.

This was always Mom's cue to serve supper. It's not that she favored eating while Darby was performing his nightly absolutions, but she knew that if we were sitting down at the kitchen table we wouldn't be able to see our neighbor lighten the load of his day.

To my mother's relief, Darby was regular … at least in his schedule. Mom could time four hamburgers to come off the broiler just as Darby was coming out onto his back porch. By the time he hit the first step the cheese would be melting and just as we'd bow our heads to say, "Lord we thank you for this food, pardon us many sinners in Christ's name. Amen," Darby would be lowering his drawers.

We weren't the only family who prayed when Darby dumped. What started out as an amusing enough small town eccentricity soon became the shame of the village. The town board even hired a lawyer to draw up an ordinance against Darby's nightly ceremony, but each time the young man brought back the new language the boys on the board would either veto it because he wasn't being plain enough or laugh it off the agenda when he was.

Darby must have been over seventy when I first became aware of him. His general store was right next to the Reel Brothers Groceries, Feed and Sundries, and you couldn't buy a sundry without going past Darby's. I never knew what sundries were, but if you had to pass Darby's store to get them, then I'd just do without.

The Reel Brothers had the finest general store in the county and they managed to maintain the turn-of-the-century charm long after supermarkets had driven their kind out of business. Hank Reel had studied art at the University of Chicago then returned to paint primitives for the rest of his life while working in the meat department, building boats in his basement and collecting Indian artifacts. Riley was the business end of the partnership and Carl was a glad-hander who'd greet you at the door and make you feel truly glad you came to shop. They installed silent alarms in the store that would ring in the boys' homes when an intruder entered in the middle of the night. The store had been robbed three times in my lifetime and they had killed two men while defending Reel Brothers Groceries, Feed & Sundries. Their method was simple and crook-proof. Riley and Carl would enter the front door with twelve-gauge shotguns, make a great deal of commotion, and Hank would be waiting near the loading dock in the back of the store. He'd give the robbers a chance to stop, and if they passed up this opportunity, he'd shoot them … usually in flight as they peddled the air coming off the loading dock. Two men killed, three wounded, and none got away … at least for long.

Local poet and horse trader Richard Laird once wrote a song about the Reel boys and their last robbery. "Bad man went a-runnin' 'cross the Illinois bottom. Couldn't find his buddy, 'cause Hank Reel had shot 'im."

The Reels had a polite but tenuous relationship with Darby Sitton. They shared the same brick wall between their two buildings, and the Reels knew that if they didn't keep the joint wall and roof in shape, Darby wasn't about to. Whenever the roofers would appear, Carl Reel would smile and say, "Just keep movin' east over Darby's place and we'll pay for that, too."

Darby might have stood maybe five foot four if he'd ever straightened up, but to my memory, he didn't. He would tamp his pipe down with a charge of Prince Albert, light it up, then go charging … head-down as if fighting a strong wind, for the four blocks to his store. He wore the same grey shirt with his long johns showing under the bottom of each sleeve, stained gray pants, and an old, sweat-stained gray cap that was still stained a good seven years after Darby quit sweating. He'd unlock the gray padlock on his gray door and that's the last you'd see of him all day unless you had some reason to shop at Darby's. I never did. I never knew anyone who did. Dad said that the shelves were filled with food in crumbling boxes and mice ran freely over the smiling Quaker's head on the oatmeal containers.

I had no idea how Darby spent his day, but my young imagination conjured up visions of the old man mixing potions and boiling cats. Some said he read old newspapers, slept, and counted his money.

Darby Sitton had lots of money. This was more than a rumor … we knew it to be a fact because most of his money was once in the pocketbooks of the rest of the town. As my grandpa explained it to me, when the Great Depression hit, Darby was the only man in town who had money and he commenced to buy up everything that the local farmers and businessmen wanted to sell. At one time Darby owned five teams of horses. This was unheard of during the Depression. Nobody owned five teams, but Darby did. All of the horses slowly starved to death under Darby's watch.

My Dad was a reasonable person and a man of peace, but the horse-starving episode stretched even his good graces. You didn't hurt a horse when Dad was around. He once fired a blacksmith who slapped my mare when she shied away from his hot horseshoe. Our horses never felt a bit in their mouths, simply the Hackamore chain under their chin. When we'd watch one of those old western movies where they'd purposely trip horses to make them appear to be shot during an Indian raid, Dad would jump up and turn off the TV set. "Boy, that's hard on horses," he'd say.

The Freemasons were forced to sell their temple to Darby and he quickly let it fall into such a state of disrepair that the county declared it a safety hazard. "But," said Grandpa, "that's all you could do during the Depression … just declare things hazards … nobody had the money to do anything about it."

Darby once owned a dozen cars all parked in the junk pile that was his back yard. He was the town's pawnshop. When your credit got so bad you could no longer feed your family, you sold Darby your car … or your washing machine or your house. And when you got a bit more flush, Darby often wouldn't sell it back. Men would load up in a wagon then go to Valley Draw to get drunk, and while at the Riverview Bar they'd vow to kill Darby for his greediness and waste, but by the time they'd made the 17-mile trip back to Homerville, they'd either be sober or passed out.

Rupert Dodds once made a deal with Darby to buy his wife's sewing machine for just a day. The few banks that survived the Depression weren't loaning any money, and Rupert needed 12 dollars fast to make a house payment. Darby took the old sewing machine, gave Rupert the 12 dollars, and then watched him hurry off to the bank to save the house. Times being what they were, Rupert wasn't able to pay off Darby until four days later. When he walked into the store, cash in hand, Darby refused to sell him the machine back. He said that Rupert had reneged on the deal.

Rupert Dodds was a big German farmer. Honest, strong, and Lutheran to the bone. But according to my Dad, on that hot August afternoon Rupert cried like a baby as he left Darby's store. Melba Dodd's sewing was all that was keeping the family alive and there was no way in the world Rupert could afford to buy her a new machine.

I suppose that today we would have found a way to have Darby committed to an asylum, but in those days his malady was labeled just plain meanness. Melba's sewing machine rusted away in the front window of Darby's store underneath a patch of roof that Reel's roofers had somehow missed.

Which is in no way to say that Darby was dishonest. You don't need to be a crook if you've got enough money. Your cash on hand does the robbing for you. When I'd ask Dad how God or the government could allow such a man to walk around free and unharmed, Dad would tell me that meanness might be sin but that it wasn't against the law.

Like most boys in Homerville, I had no great desire to meet Darby face to face. I'd much rather take the coward's way … spy and dash. Our group of boys would watch Darby come puffing up the street like a toy locomotive and dare each other to hold our ground the longest. None of us could hold out for less than a block. He scared us.

The old man had no tooth in his head as far as we could tell, his face and chin were perpetually covered with tobacco-stained gray stubble, and no one had ever seen his eternally squinted right eye. He was Popeye on the day Bluto had won. Some said he never washed, but our family knew this to be a lie. … at least in the summertime. Darby kept his washtub on his back porch and his summer baths were as immodest as his nightly defecations. He'd enter the washtub from the west, giving us the rearward view. The old man had no butt. None. It just wasn't there. I'd seen a butt like it in social studies class when Mr. Heck brought out some old photos of concentration camp survivors and can remember the collective gasp that went up from our eighth-grade class as we envisioned drifting off into old age without benefit of buttocks.

My brother Kelly was the first in our family to notice Darby's butt-less-ness. Kelly was reenacting Custer's last stand with the help of peach branches on our cellar door when he gazed toward Sitting Bull's territory and saw Darby standing stark naked on his back porch. Tossing down his rifle and commanding his troops to stand at ease, Kelly went running inside to Mom.

"Mom, Darby's naked on the back porch."

Mother peered out the kitchen window. "Oh, dear Lord."

"He lost his butt, Mom."

"Just stay inside 'til he's done."

"What happened to it?"

"What happened to what?"

"His butt. He was born with one wasn't he? Don't ever'body got a butt?"

"How about some cookies?"

"Can I take some to Darby?"

"Not now. Wait 'til he dries off … and … covers himself."

Our family was good to Darby, I think. At least as good as he'd allow us to be. We took him a basket of cookies and candy at Christmas and we'd mow the strip of his yard closest to ours. Darby owned several mowers, all bought up during the Depression, but he used none of them. Dad would often offer him a ride to his store when the snow got deep, and Darby would always be glad to hop in. Dad said that it was a short drive and he could always roll the windows down when Darby's smell got too important to ignore. Winters put a clamp on Darby's hygiene. Dad never smoked his cigar in the truck except when he'd give Darby a ride uptown. Then he smoked a lot.

Homerville was the third-smallest town in Pike County but it had the widest main street for six counties. The main drag was a half city block wide punctuated by a bandstand right in the middle of the boulevard. At its bustling biggest, somewhere around the turn of the century, its businesses straddled each side of the main street for a long block in each direction. Darby's general store was located right at the center of mercantile district, flanked on one side by the Reel brothers and on the other by Hap Lyman's lumber yard. Darby's was said to be the oldest store in town and although we had no way of proving it, it certainly looked like the oldest store. It shouted Old! as you passed. A tin awning out front dared three metal struts to hold it up, three display windows with years of grease and dust hid the store's contents, a double screen door refused to budge on the bottom without a kick, and the entire building had resisted painting since the day it was built.

From Darby's store the old man could step out and gaze west at the cemetery on the hill or east toward the highway. This is why Darby's daddy, Riley Sitton, put the store smack dab in the middle of Homerville's future. In those days it was trade and barter, with little real cash ever trading hands. When you'd come to town on Wednesday or Saturday night, you could buy whatever

Riley Sitton had purchased that afternoon. Eggs were a hot commodity and always tradable, but whole hogs and sides of beef were accepted just as readily. Riley carried his entire life savings in a brown leather wallet tucked inside his shirt. He was of the opinion that if anyone was man enough to whip him for it, it'd do him no good anyway since he'd have to be dead.

Unlike the scrawny Darby, Riley was a big old Irishman. His nose was bulbous from years of snooting the grape, and his bloodshot face looked like a roadmap of the Missouri foothills. And stubborn. My grandpa told me of the time when a cigar-smoking farmer got into an argument with Riley about whether or not he'd returned his egg crates. Grandpa claimed that the two men moved closer and closer as the argument became more heated, and when they finally stopped approaching each other, the hot ash of the farmer's cigar was touching the tip of Riley's whiskey nose. Riley didn't back off an inch. The nose began to smolder and still Riley held his ground.

Riley had seven sons. Six of them he beat so badly that they left home soon after they dirtied their last diaper, and the seventh, Darby, he taught to be a businessman. Darby was the youngest of the tribe and the neighbors just assumed that the old man found he wasn't having any luck with the belt strap and decided on education for his final spurt.

When Darby's friends were playing basketball in the haymow of Bob Brimley's barn, Darby was practicing the art of long division. When the boys hit Pete White's pasture for spring baseball, Darby was learning the principles of hog futures on the Chicago Mercantile Exchange. Darby didn't need an adding machine, although he had bought an old Singer model from J.D. Lahr when the meat locker went out of business. He could slide your groceries across the oak counter and add the figures in his head as fast as you could throw them his way. Darby was never off so much as a penny.

This was all in his better days. Now he left the store twice a day … once to puff down to the post office for his Wall Street Journal, and once to go home. I doubt that he got a half-dozen customers a year in his last decade of the grocery business. Oh, an occasional heckler would stop by to razz him when the Cardinals beat the Cubs, knowing that Darby proclaimed loud and long that Cardinal fans were only welcome in his store if they kept their mouths shut about baseball. He was not above threatening to kill Cardinal fans but his rants were generally laughed off. Grandpa told me that "Cub fans, like the Jews, deserve an extra break considering what all they've had to go through."

The winter nights would come quick and I'd peer out the window at Darby's lightless house and ask Dad what Darby was doing.

"Sleeping, I imagine. He goes to bed at sunset."

"But I mean … all alone like that? Don't you reckon he gets lonesome?"

"Some folks can do without company. I guess Darby's one of 'em."

Dad always had sympathy for Darby … except when he starved the horses.

One night my brother and I were in the yard trying to see how many fireflies it'd take to make a lantern of our Mason jar when we heard the most eerie sound coming from the upstairs of Darby's house.

"What you reckon that was?" my brother asked me.

"Don't know. Was it a giggle?"

"Darby? Darby's gigglin'? At what?"

"Don't know. I guess he's countin' other folks' money."

I remember that night because it was the evening before Darby died.

The next night we had just sat down to supper when Dad looked out and saw a car pulling slowly down the incline in front of Darby's house. The car wound down to a stop and we heard what sounded like a snap of a branch in a high wind. Then, the car moved on.

The shot caught Darby in the stomach and at first he thought it was his ulcer. The damned thing had plagued him for years but he wasn't about to pay a doctor to tell him what he already knew. Darby had served in the war and seen men die, and it never occurred to him that a gunshot could cause such little pain.

Then he saw the blood dripping down between his legs and he grabbed at his stomach.

He still didn't quite realize what was happening until he stuck his finger right in the bullet hole and figured this was to be more serious than he'd first imagined. It was a quiet musing he had with himself in those last moments. "I'll be damned," he muttered, and he stuck the finger in again. He had indeed been shot in the stomach and there was no one more amazed at this than Darby Sitton.

But the pain was still tolerable and he thought that if he could just stand up and pull up his pants, he could probably make it to his house … or better yet, our house. The bullet had evidently hit something valuable because the flow of blood now pulsed with the same regularity as Darby's racing heart. But here was the problem … he found he could not stand. The hot tip of lead had severed a portion of Darby's spine and he simply could not get his legs to pay any attention to what his brain was trying to tell them.

"Darby on his throne tonight, Dad?" I asked.

"I s'pect he is. It's suppertime."

"Can I look?"

"No, you may not," said Mother. "Eat your goulash. You're the one who always wants goulash when it snows."

"Snow?" My brother spent his entire young life in the present and never knew of such things as weather forecasts. "It's snowin'?"

"Been snowin' for ten minutes," said Dad.

Kelly made a move for the door. "Not 'til you eat supper!" said Mom. "The snow will last, Kelly. It'll hit the ground then it'll stay there." We all laughed. Every family must have a youngest child to say the stupid things that we've all thought.

Kelly's nose was out of joint. We'd gone over the kidding limit. He stuck out his lower lip and crossed his arms. Mom relented, "Okay kiddo, take a peek out the window. Just a peek, then get back to that goulash."

In a heartbeat, Kelly had dragged his chair to the window over the sink and was leaning dangerously toward the lemon lush dessert. "Wow! It really is snow!"

"No kiddin', Kelly? It ain't butter or whipped cream this time?"

But the advent of the season's first snow deafened his ears to my kidding. "It's … I mean, it's just all over the place! It's …" and he stopped. "Dad, what's a matter with Darby?"

Mother rose, "That's enough, young man. I told you to look at the snow, not that old man …" But she stopped. Her tone changed. "Get down from there." Her eyes never left the window as she whispered, " Lawrence, come here."

Dad knew that tone. He got up quickly and peered out the window. A silence, then, "Oh hell."

Once … only once before had I ever heard Dad cuss. It was late one July night when he had answered the phone then slowly sank into his chair, holding his head in his hands. He quietly whispered, "Oh, my God." His good friend James had been found on the levee of his pond, a Ford 8N tractor on top of him.

When Kelly heard Dad say, "Oh hell," he started to cry. Kelly had no idea what was going on, but he knew it was bad and that his chances of playing in the season's first snowfall had just been knocked down a notch.

"Everybody stay inside," and Dad was out the back door. Mom watched from the kitchen, gently patting the top of Kelly's sobbing head.

"What is it, Mom?" I asked.

"I don't know. Your dad will tell us when he gets back."

Dad hurdled what was left of Darby's woven-wire chicken fence in a single leap and carefully rushed up the wooden steps. Darby had fallen forward onto the few remaining inches of platform and his body was dangerously close to falling into his dung pit. Dad looked for a clean or at least a clothed spot of Darby to grab onto and finally took hold of the back of Darby's shirt. He flopped the lifeless, half-naked body of Darby over onto its back and saw that Darby's left forefinger was stuck up to the knuckle into his own stomach. The blood had begun to dry on his crotch and thighs.

Death by gunshot was not anybody's first guess in Homerville and it wasn't Dad's that night. Autopsies were expensive and we all just assumed that the crazy old man had gone

to empty his bowels, then for some reason stuck his finger into the thin skin on his stomach and died. By the time Jimmy Dodds confessed to the killing some forty years later, it was too late to be digging up Darby again and confirming anything.

Jimmy Dodds moved away from Homerville in 1939 after his family was forced to sell their farm. Jimmy had done well as a machinist in Decatur, raised a family, and was two weeks short of being dead with lung cancer. In the letter to his niece in St. Louis he said, "Darby Sitton killed my father or might as well have. He wouldn't give back Mom's sewing machine and that was our only hope of making a living. When Dad died that winter there was only one man to blame and that was old man Sitton. I'm sorry I did it. I confess my sin to you since I don't for sure know how to tell the story to my own kids. I just had to tell somebody. If there was ever a reason for killing somebody, it was this one. Some people need killing."

"Darby Sitton, killed by a sewing machine, December 12th, 1953." Or least that's the way Dad puts it. Greed was more the cause, I suppose. And meanness. No matter what they tell you, meanness kills.

The Freemason bought back their lodge hall, the Reel Brothers bought the old store and tore it down, the lot where Darby's house stood is now one of the nicest split-level homes in Homerville, and the town doesn't even have a grocery store. You can look from one end of Homerville to the other and you'll not find a trace of Darby Sitton. No matter what they tell you, meanness kills.

Homerville

The first glacier gave birth to Homerville, Illinois, 150,000 years ago as a continent of ice swallowed up everything southward to St. Louis. When the ice beat its melting retreat northward, it coughed up Homerville and left the town's present topography … a clump of rich, black dirt. Another few thousand years of wind and rain rounded the hillocks to the town's present landscape before the big glacier's little brother, some 140,000 years later, stopped at Peoria, ignoring Homerville completely. But its melting floods carved out the nearby Illinois River Valley and forced the Mississippi River to jump to its present location.

Homerville ... nine streets north and south, three and a piece east and west, with a few trees older than the western states. The town was a history of Western Illinois in miniature. Once a thriving little settlement of commerce and trade, it was now the final home of retired men who still wore "real work pants" instead of bluejeans, women who got their hair done once a week, and just enough younger families to make a grade school worthwhile.

The major exports of Homerville were long-told stories, way too many tomatoes, and a few decent basketball players. Twenty years ago the town's death was sagely predicted by anyone who cared to think about such things but that was before the entire Midwest began retiring. If you'd done well and had no kin to keep you around, you went to Arizona. If your wife had inherited enough to get you by, you moved to Texas. The rest moved off the farm and into two-story frame houses in Homerville and hoped that Social Security lasted at least a day longer than they did.

Situated as it was on the rolling glacial hills, you couldn't view the town in a single glance. The town dipped a bit on its western end while the eastern edge rolled on toward the Illinois River.

These were not city folks who retired to a quaint little place on the prairie or young upward couples in search of small town life for their children. The typical resident of Homerville was raised within twenty miles of the town and didn't play golf, wear baby blue shorts with black socks to mow his yard, or subscribe to USA Today. He went to church, consumed a great deal of coffee, and once had a relative who drank too much. Porch swings were still in abundance but the blessed twentieth-century conjunction of air conditioning and color television had pretty much left the swings unmanned unless the weather was especially fine and the summer reruns smothered the broadcast schedule.

Homerville was mainly Protestant. Oh, they'd seen Catholics and heard a good deal about them, but the Methodists and Presbyterians pretty much took top spot on any census with the Church of Christ soaking up what was left. The town was strangely

Democratic in party preference for no known reason other than the fact that their fathers had voted Democrat. The Presbyterians and the Church of Christ were housed in straight-a-by-God-head New England style structures while the Methodists worshipped in a homier, rounded, Southern-style church. The churches met together once a year as they played taps over the departed Veterans on Memorial Day and then gathered again for Easter Sunrise breakfast. Eventually the Church of Christ dwindled to but a handful of progressive souls who began walking over to worship with the Presbyterians, in spite of the fact that their new church used a live piano. The Methodists were the only group in town who could afford a fulltime minister and even that dwindled to circuit rider status of late.

The town had no Golden Gate Bridge or Sears Tower but it did have the bandstand standing right in the middle of Main Street. Not alongside Main or in the park beside Main, it was in the middle of the street and was erected in 1921 by Johnny Johnson, right on the site of the previous bandstand which was on the site of the town well and horse tank. The eight-sided gazebo seemed to lord over the geography as you approached up the hill from the west and you could see all the way down Main when you pulled off the highway some six blocks east.

You didn't need to be terribly old to remember the hitching posts lining the business district's eastern stretch, and most residents at the café can attest to having handled a two-horse team. Some of the older residents still kept horses as a sort of rich man's hobby and the Methodists made a regular thing of hitching Phil Jackson's Percherons to a wagon on Christmas Eve then trotting around the town singing carols. One of Phil's horses was asked to fly to California to be in the movie *Sea Biscuit*. Most folks in town own the video tape.

The town meets in convocation three times a day for morning coffee, lunch and then again for afternoon coffee. The ladies command the front of the café and the men inhabit the rear. Anyone sitting at the side tables is either newly married or from out of town. The café is closed on Mondays so the Methodists serve lunch for all faiths, Presbyterians paying the same as everyone else. The ladies occupy the front part of the fellowship hall and the men sit in the back near the kitchen.

Anybody with half a brain is asleep by 10:30 and only a fool or a minister would dare sleep past 7. The town seems to be waiting but for nothing in particular. It's a good place to wait and will continue to be so until the next glacier comes along.

The last glacier left a good sixty inches of powdery loess on Homerville and then organic topsoil was added at the rate of one inch every thousand years. The town sits 700 feet above sea level. In another thousand years it will have changed about that much.

The Piano Teacher

Marietta LaTeur's pencil came down across Keith's fingers. "Like a rake. I've told you like a rake, not a … well, a hammer."

The round little boy tried again to curve his stubby fingers into an arc, a position totally unsuited to his ten little nubs. Again he broke headlong into The *Spinning Wheel Song*. He winced as she again tapped her pencil on the back of his knuckles. "You will never," intoned Marietta, "achieve any dexterity … any speed or fluency if you persist in holding your fingers flat like that. Now begin again."

"Where?"

"At the beginning, of course."

Marietta's next student was waiting on the end stool of the restaurant counter and Keith Orr was going to be the rest of the evening mastering the *Spinning Song*. She'd let him finish this time. She thought she saw a tear in his left eye and she certainly didn't want to send him home crying … again.

Marietta LaTeur's piano studio was the far corner of the backroom of the last business on the south side of Main … The Village Inn, one of the town's two restaurants. Nina Houston bought the store from Ray and Lavonia Hannel when Ray was killed in a Christmas Eve accident when the sewer line he was repairing caved in on him. We saw him die on live television.

Channel Ten had their camera stuck down in the hole on Broadway and 12th in Quincy, trying to interview the trapped municipal worker. Ray was a Homerville boy and everybody in town was watching his black and white Zenith with every intention of witnessing a heartwarming Christmas Eve rescue. We could see Ray's mud-smudged face as Hal Barton stuck his NBC microphone into the pit, then there was a rustling noise, somebody shouted and Ray closed his eyes. It was a special event since the television usually went off shortly after ten but the technical crew from Channel 10 had stayed with Ray in the pit so they kept the station on the air until about 1 a.m. when Ray died. Dead on live television. We'd never seen anything like it until Jack Ruby shot Lee Harvey Oswald live and on some sets, in color.

Marietta LaTeur lived up over the "Ferd and Rob's Barbershop," and on summer Sunday mornings you'd hear her practicing the church hymns all up and down Main Street. She was the pianist for the Presbyterians until Preacher DeVry came to town and insisted on purchasing the new hymnal with more upbeat tunes. Marietta didn't go so far as to assign snappier hymns to the work of Satan, but she was sure they had been written somewhere south of heaven. So, for the past 17 years she'd accompanied the Methodist brethren and sistren, a congregation that was never in any danger of being tainted by progress.

Her teaching studio was rented from Nina at a dollar a week, a token sum since Nina was going to heat the room anyway and if the truth were known, Nina would have paid Marietta to teach there. Her piano lessons not only provided some uneven but interesting music each afternoon and for most of the day Saturday, but it guaranteed a steady clientele of parents waiting to pick up their aspiring pianists. The lighting was terrible but Marietta didn't complain. If you slowly moved your music across the piano to keep in line with the setting sun shining in the back door, *The Spinning Wheel Song* could look quite glorious on the page, no matter how it sounded.

Keith finally spun out on *The Spinning Wheel Song* and turned on his piano stool to face the music. "Well," sighed Marietta, "you made it and nobody died." Keith smiled. Miss

LaTeur was a demanding teacher but she could be funny. In fact, he liked her quite a lot, which was an amazing accomplishment since he completely and thoroughly hated the piano. "A red star," said Marietta. "That wasn't a blue star performance." Keith was satisfied. He'd had white stars for the last two weeks, and not only were they the lowest rank you could possibly get, they didn't show up on the white pages of his *John Thompson Piano Book, Second Book, Purple Edition.*

Marietta patted him on the head and he was more than happy to scoot out the room and run on to Little League practice. He hated it when he came in late to baseball practice. The coach knew he'd be late on Mondays and that was fine. In fact, the coach often forgot Keith was on the team. But the other players would give him a good hoot when he tried to sneak into his right field position late.

Marietta raised her beautiful soprano voice and sang out, "Carole? Are you there?" Carole was a voice student and a welcome break from two hours of stubby, untalented fingers. At least Carole could sing. Marietta's still-nimble fingers splashed out a G Major 7th arpeggio and Carole lit into *The Lost Chord.* Marietta closed her eyes, so glad to no longer be scraping the bottom of the barrel.

Her father would strip little Marietta down to her underthings then stretch the red leotard over her tiny body before cramming her into the barrel. Marietta always had to go in first since she was the smallest. Then he'd lower Petey in on top of her as she tucked herself into a crumpled little ball. Frankie was lowered down on top of Pete, then Margaret, then Marietta's mother, and finally Harry LaTeur himself climbed in on top of his wife to complete the family package. He'd whisper "Now" to the stage manager and the old man would tip the barrel onto its side and give it a shuffling roll out onto the stage as the band broke into *Side by Side*.

The band would suddenly stop playing once the barrel reached the very edge of the orchestra pit. The audience would always go silent, thinking that perhaps some stagehand had made a mistake and knocked an oak barrel onto the stage. Then, just as the silence was becoming uncomfortable, Harry LaTeur would stick his head out of the top of the tipsy cask. He always wore his "Toby" face for this act, rosy cheeks, huge exaggerated freckles, and a red dot on the end of his nose. The audience would roar with laughter as the limber-legged man would crawl out of the barrel, peer back into the barrel's cavernous mouth, shrug, then reach in to pull out Mrs. LaTeur in her "Suzy" costume … the same red freckles and cheeks, but with an huge overdrawn mouth of lipstick. The two would do a knock-about routine with Mrs. L complaining about being cramped up in the barrel, then just as she was about to chase Toby offstage, Margaret would stick her head out of the barrel and shout a blood-curdling, "Heeeeeelp!" Toby would do a shock-take to the audience then run to pull her out, and grabbing desperately to Margaret's legs would be Pete and as the mama and papa clown kept pulling children out of the barrel, Frankie would pop out, hanging onto Pete's suspenders. The audience would roar as each successive LaTeur poured out of their tiny rolling home.

Frankie did a crying baby bit and Harry would pretend to whip him with a large rubber bottle, causing Mama Clown to throw a fit, jumping up and down so hard she'd lose her bloomers while Margaret and Pete played peek-a-boo with the drummer. It was pure slapstick and always a guaranteed belly laugh in the early days of Vaudeville. But the act had a Jim-dandy topper as the family would take their final bow then leave the stage. Just when the audience thought they'd seen the climax, Marietta would crawl out of the barrel with a large pacifier in her mouth, do a cute-take to the audience, and crawl off. The LaTeur Players were always in demand and although they never got top billing, they often opened the second act … as prime a position as a family act ever achieved.

Carole took the repeat in the music and had just begun with,

Seated one day at the organ …
I was weary and ill at ease …
And my fingers wondered idly
Over the noisy keys …

Harry LaTeur was born Harry Jankowski, a first generation Pole fresh off the boat from Warsaw. He landed in New Orleans with a harmonica and winning enough smile to get him a job in The Dark Lady Rendezvous on a nightly basis. He charmed his way up the Mississippi one summer, playing the lounge on a political junket, and when he landed in Hannibal he met Marilyn and married her within the week. He wrote back to his mother in Poland that he had intended to sail far enough into the country to meet America's most beautiful woman then marry her. And that's what he did.

Vaudeville was hot in those days, and so was Harry LaTeur. The result was four kids and a booking on the Great Pantages Circuit. Radio was barely known, the movies and television were still years away from public consumption, and Vaudeville was king. Vaudeville was for everyone. Everyone could afford a ticket, and you laughed at the German comics whether you understood them or not, the Italian juggler amazed you without knowing his language, and the French contortionist needed no words to drop your jaw. A jumbled soup of nationalities was being stirred on the stage as the rest of the country applauded. The Vaudeville performer wasn't the least bit picky about who was in his audience and the audiences were similarly tolerant as to who mounted the stage that night.

Marietta and her family were part of an explosion. In the 1920's there were 20,000 Vaudeville acts in the country and over 2 million people in the audience every day. Nine or ten acts would constitute a Vaudeville bill and if you were good enough, you were picked up for circuit work, guaranteeing you a place to play for up to a year's work without looking for a new act. The LaTeur players once worked a month in California with the legendary Dolly Sisters and did a two-week engagement in St. Louis with Helen Keller heading the bill. Harry LaTeur loved Vaudeville since, unlike variety shows, they were guaranteed to be clean, and that's just what he wanted for his children. The LaTeurs (that season called *The Flying LaTeurs*) once did a ten-month tour with the Keith and Albee Circuit. Posted near the stage door was a sign that read:

Don't say "slob" or "son of a gun" or "hully gee" on the stage unless you want to be canceled peremptorily. Do not address anyone in the audience in any manner. If you do not have the ability to entertain Mr. Keith's audience without risk of offending them, do the best you can. Lack of talent will be less open to censure than would be an insult to a patron. If you are in doubt as to the character of your act consult the local manager before you go on stage, for if you are guilty of uttering anything sacrilegious or even suggestive you will be immediately closed and will never again be allowed in a theatre where Mr. Keith is in authority.

And that was just the way Harry LaTeur wanted it. There was to be no blue material in his family's act or any act they'd ever be allowed to watch. (It was the Mr. Keith who originated the term "blue material." If your act was in any was offensive, you'd receive a blue envelope in your drop box, warning you what to cut and often containing suggestions for revising the material.) Marietta remembered that her young days were filled with morning lessons in arithmetic and spelling from Mama, while the afternoon belonged to Papa … juggling, voice lessons, acrobatics, mimicry, rope twirling, all manner of musical instruments, dance … both classical and popular, elocution and what Papa called extra-sensory levitation, an act that Marietta never understood and the audiences never fully appreciated.

Carole had finished *The Lost Chord* and was heading full-steam into *Ave Maria* when her time ran out and Miss LaTeur stopped the lesson. Carole was an alto and Marietta secretly believed that soprano was the only true female voice. They were nice enough people, but no one ever wrote a great role for an alto. She was glad to have the lesson ended. "Thank you, Carole. You know, some day I will have to pay good money to hear you sing." In the meantime, Marietta took Carole's fifty cents and watched the proud little lady run back out front to where her family was meeting her for their weekly Monday night tenderloins and French fries.

Marietta seldom ate at the Village Inn. Her little apartment had a cook stove and a small icebox. She enjoyed people, but she'd rather not eat around them. When Marietta wasn't listening to music or making music, she read. In fact, she was nearly the sole customer of Harold Bright's bookstore. She enjoyed Harold very much because he didn't like to talk, and since she was similarly adverse to chitchat, they had some truly wonderful conversations, each knowing that the other would need to have something terribly important to say or they wouldn't say it.

Marietta enjoyed music, reading, and church. Oh, not the noisy denominations that would raise their hands and shout aloud when not called upon, or the type of congregations who seemed to attend worship only to hear themselves instead of the still, small voice of God. Marietta believed that God could only be found in silence and so that's where she sought him. Some called her a prude, but she felt that to be unfair. After all, she wasn't judging anyone. She simply felt that if anything in life should be a person's own prerogative, it was her mode of worship. Period.

She did yearn for friends with a similar artistic bent but the town had only one real artist, Harry Reel at the grocery store, and Marietta could never engage him much about art. He loved to talk about his subject matter … Indians, wagon trains, scouts and Southwestern sunsets, but as to the process of painting, well … he claimed he didn't know much. He just painted, and pretty well, Marietta allowed. Then there was Heidi Engel, but she was nutty and probably not an artist at all. Marietta never knew for certain and she cared even less. It was enough burden being unmarried and artistic in a small town … she didn't want to add a certified lunatic friend to her list of suspicious attributes.

Crystal Storm came in late. Crystal was always late, her nose was always running, and she always had an excuse for not having practiced during the week. Marietta used to upbraid Crystal for her slovenly ways and wasting her parents' good money on piano lessons, until it became clear that Crystal's parents were just as confounded by her lack of both talent and responsibility and that's why they sent her for piano lessons … to learn discipline at the hands of the town's greatest musician and moral bulldog.

She'd actually heard herself referred to as that … the town's moral bulldog. It made Marietta smile. The only bulldog she'd ever known was far from moral. His name was Max.

She first met Max when the LaTeurs were a part of a southern tour and had landed in Biloxi for a three-day stand. Three-day stands were quite wonderful because you had time to catch up on your washing and for three days you toted nothing up and down hotel staircases. And the pay was the same. In 1910 the average factory worker earned less that $1,300 a year, but even a small-time Vaudeville performer playing a 42-week season, would rake in $3150 at seventy-five bucks a week. Harry LaTeur was never a Top Banana onstage, but he had a more important talent … business. Marietta's father was a bull of a man who intimidates you at 8 o'clock, charms you at nine, and fast-talks you into a prime billing by 10. Although Harry could hold his own onstage, his best performances were saved for the smoke-soaked offices of the booker.

Max was a part of Kate Karlson's Calamitous Canines, a dog act that enjoyed some popularity in the late twenties. No group was harder to maintain on the Vaudeville circuit since dogs would age, dogs would get sick, dogs would die, and then there was Max who spent his performing days in a lusty search for sex. It was not unusual for audience members to bring their pets into a performance and more than once Marietta had seen the opening trick in Kate Karlson's Calamitous Canines interrupted when Max would gaze out into row three, sniff a bitch in heat and take off up the aisle leaving some poor female patron screaming after her Pomeranian, the audience roaring with delight, and Kate's "Bulldog Jumps the Ring of Fire" a complete burnout.

Max was worse backstage. He had an inordinate desire for anything long and cylindrical … pillows, sandbags, and his greatest object of desire seemed to be the wooden leg of Wanda, Contortionist Extraordinaire. Wanda was perhaps the only one-legged female contortionist in the history of Vaudeville and of course had no feeling in her artificial limb. She'd be lying backstage limbering up on her red velvet blanket when she'd notice a desperate umph-umph-umph sound and feel her leg bouncing on the velvet. She'd look down and see Max humping her leg, eyes closed, and oblivious to the world of Vaudeville.

Then, when Berg Clifford called Marietta a moral bulldog after she took her stand against voting Homerville "wet," ... well, she had to laugh.

Crystal's piano lesson ended in tears. It always ended in tears. Most students talked of codas, key signatures, and accidentals. Crystal would whine about her load of homework, her stomachaches, and the fact that nobody appreciated her. With Crystal sobbing Marietta would rub her back a bit, stroke her pony-tailed hair, and assure her that she would get her homework done, her stomachache would eventually go away and she was indeed loved. Ten minutes of piano and twenty minutes of therapy … that was about the quota for Crystal, and Marietta supposed it was time well spent. Crystal was never going to become a musician but she would eventually grow to become a human being, and if that's how the two ladies were to spend their time together then so be it. Marietta asked Crystal if she'd like to lick the blue star herself. "Blue star, Miss LaTeur? I've never got me a blue star before!"

"You deserve one today," Marietta lied, then gave Crystal a hug that she was sure would carry her home. Two more lessons and Marietta would be able to walk next door to the barbershop, climb the stairs, and have supper. Marietta carefully timed her lessons so she'd only walk through the barbershop after closing hours. Ferd and Rob's Barbershop was an all-male bastion and although it didn't bother her a whit to traipse through, it put the barbers and their patrons into an uncomfortable panic. Ferd would always be in mid-obscenity when Miss LaTeur came through and since he was nearly blind, brother Rob would shout "Evening, Miss LaTeur!" to warn him. Woe be it unto the hapless head that Ferd would be barbering when he heard this. The trick was to grab your ears and duck.

"And how's my favorite student?" sang Marietta as Tommy Marshall skipped through the restaurant door, piano book in hand. Tommy was indeed her prize student. If any of her young charges would someday be known for his musicianship, it would surely be

Tommy. His fingers were long and almost feminine … in fact, much about Tommy was almost feminine, and it gave him a sensibility so lacking in most of her students. Tommy plopped onto the piano stool and smiled at her through his metal-clad teeth, his mop of dark hair bouncing with excitement. Tommy's piano lesson was the highlight of his week and certainly a relief for Miss LaTeur.

"And what will it be today?" asked Marietta. She always let Tommy choose his own pieces.

"Hungarian Rhapsody Number Two ... in C-sharp minor!"

"Splendid!" and Tommy would leave his book closed while he threw back his tussled head imitating the great pianists and dive headlong into Mr. Liszt's wonderful fantasy for fingers. Marietta smiled at her prize student. She heard very little of the music but she heard the more beautiful sounds of a soul breathing and finding a voice. Tommy was born too late. He could have been a Next-to-Closer.

The Vaudeville bill was always the same … A "silent" or "dumb" act would start the show … a juggler or Kate's Canines … nothing that required talking since the audience would still be entering the theatre and the act could go on despite the disturbances. The number two spot was usually a Singing Sister or Dancing Brother act although the performers were seldom related. By the time the third act was called the audience was pretty much settled so the spot was often a comedy sketch. The fourth spot was Marietta's favorite for it was here that the novelty acts got their shot. One of Marietta's favorites was Randy the Regurgitator, a fellow from Nevada who would swallow all manner of objects then bring them back up again. Another was Think-A-Drink Hoffman, a tuxedoed dandy who'd come onstage, cocktail shaker in hand, and magically pour out any drink the audience could mention. Spot Five closed Act One and it consisted of either a famous has-been or a rising wannabe fighting his way to stardom.

Act Two opened with the spot most coveted by the LaTeur family. It was traditionally know as "The Big Act," and every group wanted this position on the bill. Really good animal acts could gain this spot if all the dogs were healthy and Max had a cold bath before coming onstage … large sets, gaudy costuming, choirs and dancers. It just had to be big and Harry LaTeur knew how to beef up an act if that's what the bill required. He called it "dressing the act." Next-to-Closing was the spot for the headliner and the place Marietta envisioned the young pianist now sitting before her, digging Liszt's sixteenth-notes out of the old black piano. The "Closing Spot" in Vaudeville was usually a short movie, a really bad singer, or a one-man band … anything boring enough to encourage the patrons to leave the theatre and make room for the next audience. When you were offered the job of "closer," you knew your Vaudeville days had come to an end.

Tommy's rendition came to its end and Miss LaTeur burst into applause. He stood smartly, rested one hand on the keyboard, and took a small bow. Then Tommy threw up. He almost always vomited after a really good performance. He knew the routine and once he felt his little gorge beginning to fill, he dashed for the back door and became Tommy the Regurgitator. It only took one misplaced heave one cloudy summer evening for Tommy to realize that Lap Toosman often slept off his drunks in the grass behind the Village Inn. Tommy had just run out the door after an especially inspiring performance of *Brahms' Sonata Number One in C Major, Opus One,* when the urge hit him and he made his customary run out the back door. Miss LaTeur was just bending over to retrieve Tommy's music when she heard the distinctly un-Brahms-like sound of "What the hell? Why you little snot! What in the hell do you think you're …" and by that time, Marietta had grabbed the young virtuoso by the collar and jerked him back into the restaurant, apologizing to the besmeared Lap Toosman and telling a sobbing Tommy that it wasn't his fault. "We'll laugh about this one day, Tommy." And they did.

It was the odd moments that made Homerville such a joy for Marietta. She'd lived her life hoping for the next odd moment. Like the night Hadji Ali caught fire in Memphis. Hadji's act consisted of two parts. First he'd swallow a fishbowl of water then spit it back out into the bowl, the confused goldfish coming up last. His finale was truly grand when it worked. Hadji would spew a mouthful of gasoline onto an open flame. This delighted audiences and made him one of the most sought-after novelty acts on the Pantages Circuit. Backstage he'd coat his mouth and lips with warm paraffin to protect his tender tissues. Then he'd take a stiff drink and head toward the stage in his loincloth and Swami headpiece. Hadji had lost his share of moustaches over the years and his beard was always singed a bit, but until that night in Memphis he'd never experienced a total flameout. Marietta's father told her that the Swami had a cold that evening and his assistant mistook his signal of "Hold it a minute, I've got to cough," with "Go ahead and light the torch." Marietta was waiting in the wings in her "The Dancing LaTeurs Go To The City" costume when she heard a roar, looked up and saw Hadji engulfed in flames. He'd done more than cough up the gasoline, he coughed then inhaled to get his breath.

She ran into the still-ailing Hadji in Moline during the next season's tour. He barely had a voice and he'd gone into snake charming. She waved at him from her seat in the audience as he sat there on a bed of nails with a cobra wrapped around his neck. Hadji smiled as she seemed to mouth the words, "Hi Hadji!" Actually, she was saying, "Don't cough."

It was always Harry LaTeur's hope that Marietta would become a piano player. Hardly any groups traveled with their own pianist, leaving them to the variously hideous house musicians. The local "orchestra" could be anything from the lush sounds of a polished combo at the RKO Palace in New Orleans to a solitary drunken piano player in Boatman, Montana, who scooped manure by day and played it by night. If you were a comedian or juggler requiring no more than background accompaniment you could tolerate the musical inconsistencies of the Vaudeville circuit, but for dancers, the clown on the keyboards could make or break your act. Marietta remembered that the term "hoofers" came from dancers who would stand offstage before their entrance and stomp out the tempo like a horse pawing the ground.

Perhaps Marietta's favorite Vaudeville oddity was the Cherry Sisters. Their numbers varied from two to five and the girls were known as the worst act in Vaudeville … and one of the most highly paid, commanding a thousand dollars a week while they toured for decades. Their painfully off-key renderings of popular songs were so bad that audience members would often hurl vegetables toward the stage. A few astute theatre managers saw the possibilities in this and began to not only encourage the audience to keep hurling, but they even provided the produce. The sisters eventually had to perform from behind a net for their own safety and Marietta's father told her that the singing sisters never did realize the joke. And he added, "But they did take the money."

Harry LaTeur had no grand illusions about his little act's future and that was probably his greatest asset. Nearly every performer on the Vaudeville Circuit wanted top billing and Harry knew that no matter how many times he changed the act, his beloved little troupe were never going to be headliners. They took what work was offered them, made a good living, and were happy for it. He'd tell his little brood, "Keep your hopes in check, kids. Good ones keep you going and wrong ones kill you." And they believed him.

Harry and Marilyn LaTeur gave their children an education that no schoolroom could have afforded them, and they gathered each night for prayer, no matter how many shows they'd done that day, and no matter whether Marietta was still awake.

The last lesson of the evening had just entered the door from the restaurant. It was Marge Bartley, 78 years old and still with a dream in her head of mastering the piano. Marge always asked to go last so she'd not be seen by the children waiting for their lessons. Marietta was glad to oblige.

It was not an exaggeration to say that Marge Bartley had nearly worked herself to death. Her husband Robert was a hard-drinking railroad man who'd come home on weekends with a load of cash, wave it in her face, then do his best to beat her to death. When Marge was sufficiently bloodied and the kids had run to hide under their beds, Robert Bartley would head to Valley where he'd drink until the sun came up on Sunday morning, and when the train came through Valley they'd scoop him up off the boardwalk and he'd be gone for another week.

The sin of wife beating had a strange history in Homerville and I suppose the town was not unusual in its response. No one appreciated a wife beater and he wasn't welcome in any of the local organizations, but as to actually doing something about it … well, what should you do? What could you do? Like as not he was at least a shirttail relation to a member of every conversation in town. You could call the law and he'd get a stern warning, and then wallop her even harder next Friday night. Most towns have their secret sins and this was one that we tried our best not to think about. And that's why Marge had him killed.

Homerville always prided itself on being self-sufficient, at least in the town's heyday. A druggist, two doctors, a vet, barbershop, a variety of good places to eat, and a couple of groceries. But when Marge Bartley went looking around for hired killers she thought that maybe the town wasn't quite so self-reliant after all. We had no killers, or at least no one who advertised for the work in the *Homerville Citizen*. Where do you look? And if a man was mean enough to kill somebody, how could you ever trust him to do the job right? So she turned to her brothers.

Ralph and Willie Orville were pillars of the community, staunch Presbyterians, and a couple of the most prosperous farmers in the county. They'd raised corn, beans, beef, and children that had made them proud. When Robert Bartley was discovered head-down in his own well and Marge told the sheriff that he'd gone out to get a drink at night, stumbled drunk into the well and drowned, well … that was good enough. It did seem strange when they found he had a plug of tobacco in his mouth since men don't usually chew in their sleep, but well, that was good enough.

Marge buried him, bought a small farm with the insurance money, cash-rented the acreage, and sent her two daughters and son to college. The two girls became teachers and her son was principal at Homerville until his retirement. It took a lifetime of egg gathering, taking in washing, cleaning the neighbors' houses, and hulling pecans, but Marge got it done. Then at age 78 she gave in to her lifelong dream of playing the piano and went to see Marietta LaTeur about taking lessons.

Unlike many farm wives of the day, the years of picking, pruning, plucking, and scrubbing had kept Marge's fingers nimble and arthritis had never cast its painful spell upon her life. Marietta told her that yes, she could teach her the basics of fingering and chording … enough to play a few tunes, and that's just what she did. Of all Marietta's pupils, Marge was the most grateful for the gift of music.

Marietta's mother was like that. If she'd learned anything at all from Marilyn it was the gift of gratitude. When Harry LaTeur collapsed during a performance of "The LaTeur Family's Holiday Spectacular! Mime, Music and Merriment in a Wholesome Family Tableau" during a week's run in Indianapolis, Marilyn was grateful that he could still talk. Paralyzed from the neck down and unable to feed himself, Harry agreed to move back to Homerville, give his children their wings, and let Marilyn take care of him until he died.

Pete had made enough friends in California to work up until his sixties as a grip for Paramount Pictures, Frankie married a man from St. Louis as soon as the family moved into the apartment above the barber shop, and Margaret taught dance in Pittsfield until she formed her own little touring company of three daughters and once again there was a LaTeur Family Players on the road, albeit a county road and just during the summer.

Marietta was the baby of the family and strangely, she thought … considering how loving her parents had been to their children … the only one of the brood who seemed to feel a need to support her parents' finances. Harry LaTeur had provided a good living for the family but the idea of actually saving up any money was something he could never quite manage. When Marilyn moved him back to Homerville, he had nine hundred dollars and some change in his pocket. That was it.

Marilyn would sit at the back table of the Village Inn and hold Marietta's hand once she'd put Harry to bed for the night. "I can do laundry. I can clean houses. I didn't stop being a working housewife when I put on my Suzy makeup."

"Mother, you can't leave daddy alone. Look at you. Your hand is shaking right now because he's up there by himself."

"Marietta, I can do this. Don't think you have to …"

"I don't have to, mother. I want to. I must."

Marilyn couldn't speak. She looked into the eyes of her youngest child, the bottom of the family's rolling barrel, the baby who'd stick her head out and get the biggest laugh of the night. She squeezed Marietta's hand, shared her daughter's tears for a moment, then simply whispered, "Thank you."

At age 22, Marietta left Homerville to make a living.

"Is this really any good?" Marge was getting frustrated. "I don't think God made sharps. Flats, yes. And the key of C, but God did not make D and B and G. God did not make sharps."

Marietta smiled, "He was having a bad day, Marge. This is in G. Just one sharp. Let's try it again from the beginning."

"Are you humoring me because I'm old?"

"Yes, and I've heard you carry a gun. Now start again from the top."

Marietta looked at her reflection in the hallway mirror on the morning of her twenty-second birthday and saw a very pretty girl. She'd played a baby until she was ten and adolescent roles into her twenties. She was like her mother and would always look younger than her age. Her brother and sisters worked right alongside their parents, picking up a world of skills as they traveled from one town to the next, but Marietta had been the baby of the family. "A kept woman," her mother would joke. Now Marietta looked into the mirror and saw a very pretty woman who'd been kept from learning anything other than playing the piano.

It was a strange and almost miraculous series of events that turned demure Marietta LaTeur into "Mercy Sakes, Queen of the Burlesque Strippers." She had remembered one other skill from her family's repertoire. She knew how to capture and hold a stage.

In 1875, Ann Held, Florence Ziegfeld's first wife, disrobed behind a screen in a number called, "I'd Like To See A Little More of You," at the Mason Opera House in Los Angeles. From this first American display of flesh with musical accompaniment, striptease flourished mostly in gin joints and honkytonks. When the American public's taste turned away from Vaudeville, some customers went for the moving pictures, some the radio, and others gave a new audience to the old idea of Burlesque.

Harry LaTeur had told his children about the Burlesque houses that were giving entertainment a bad name, and he swore that his family would never perform in a place so wholly condemned by all that was holy and right and good. The LaTeur children believed this, and Marietta was probably the most adamant about keeping the family act clean and wholesome. But she had been watching.

Some of the smaller theatres ran Vaudeville during the week and on weekends turned their stage into Burlesque halls. The Depression pretty much wiped out live theatre nationwide but Burlesque thrived and moved into many of the vacant downtown venues. By 1937, seven major Broadway theatres had become Burlesque houses, and what started out as a series of parody sketches had become purely striptease.

Marietta tiptoed into her father's bedroom, looked down at the shrunken form of the man who had shown her the world and all its glories, and then quietly said to herself, "I can do this, Papa." She called a former friend in Chicago, got directions to the Fantasia Theatre, climbed on the train at Griggsville and went north to take it off.

Unlike most strippers who got into the business simply because they looked good without clothing and didn't mind letting the world know, Marietta also knew show business. She knew the tricks. Her father had always admonished her family troupe, "Leave them wanting more. Anybody will watch you once, kids. It's a pro who can bring 'em back the next night."

Marietta had no trouble getting work. A cigar-infested little man named Morris auditioned her in his office. Boobs, butt, and she had the job. Morris hadn't even asked Marietta about her act, saying simply, "Try to come up with something clever, sweetheart. And drag it out. You've got to fill twelve minutes a night." As she turned to leave, Morris said, "Hey, what's your name, kid?"

"Marietta."

"No, I mean your strip name … what's your handle?"

"Mercy sakes, I hadn't thought about that."

"Perfect. Mercy Sakes. Sounds wholesome. They'll love it."

Marietta already had her gimmick in mind and it was one that drew in the word of mouth crowd so fast that Morris raised her salary twice in the first month just to make sure she didn't think of flying off to one of the Minsky houses. Marietta played the piano.

She hired two meatpackers from the Armour plant to build a revolving stage … a circular platform twenty feet in circumference that was operated by a stagehand in each wing. They slowly pulled a long rope attached to a pulley and when Marietta sat down to play, the stage would turn, each revolution delighting her audiences with a new revelation of Marietta. She'd play *Only a Bird in A Gilded Cage*, and when Marietta would revolve upstage, the piano covering all but her head, she'd remove a item of clothing. The song took four verses and by the time she'd worked her way to verse four and she sat there in a G-string and bra, the audience would be howling for a longer song. Then, just like her daddy taught her long ago sticking her head out of the barrel, she turn to the audience and shout, "Anybody wanna hear verse five?" The roof of the Fantasia would noticeably rise each night when the audience responded. Marietta would break into the fifth verse and her circular stage would again start to revolve. Just before the blackout, the piano turned another revolution and the slobbering crowds saw Marietta playing with just her left hand, her right hand covering her bare bosom. "The perfect blackout!" Morris would exclaim every night as he fumbled in the dark to throw her a robe. "Perfect, baby! They love it!"

It takes two years of stripping, six days a week, three shows a day, to support a father paralyzed by a stroke and a mother who never bought a new dress in her life. That's just what Marietta did. She had her father's head for figures and she knew to the day just how long she'd have to show her body to drunken Chicago teamsters and out of town salesmen. Morris couldn't believe it when Marietta said she was leaving. "But baby! Baby, you've got this town by the ear! That rotatin' piano is the tops, baby! Nobody can beat that act! Nobody!" And they didn't, at least as far as Marietta LaTeur knew. She didn't care. She came home, moved in with her parents, and delighted her father by telling him about her career as accompanist to the Chicago Symphony Chorale. She had even had programs printed and Harry delighted in the concerts she'd played. "And it was you, daddy. You got me started." Harry LaTeur died happy and Marilyn moved to St. Louis to be near her grandchildren. Marietta stayed in the apartment, took in piano students, and played for church services.

Marge got up from the piano and said, "Well, I guess that's all this old sow can stand for an evening. Join me for coffee, Marietta?"

"Oh, it's getting late, Marge. Women your age should be thinking about bed."

"I could outlast you any day, girl."

"Keep dreaming, Marjorie. And think about practicing this week, will you?"

"What? And ruin my style?"

Marge put her fifty cents down on the edge of the piano. "See you next week?"

"If you're still alive."

"I'll be at your funeral, Marietta. Pro'bly playing the piano."

"And I raise up out of my coffin and give you a white star."

When Marge Bartley laughed the world shook and she laughed herself out the front door of the Village Inn. Nina stuck her head in from the kitchen. "Need anything, Marietta?"

"Just some rest, Nina. Thanks."

Marietta walked the half block to the barbershop, nodded to Ferd as he swept the day's hair from the linoleum floor. "Nice night, Miss LaTeur."

"Yes, it is, Ferd. It's a very nice night," and Marietta LaTeur went up the stairs and went to bed. Tomorrow she'd take her customary walk to the Homerville cemetery, sit by Harry's grave and they'd talk of Mustafa, the Amazing Mentalist who could never remember the number of his hotel room, of Two-Ton-Tessie The World's Only Bearded Female Wrestler who took in extra work playing Santa Claus during the holidays, and of an oaken cask that would roll out to just short of the orchestra pit before disgorging a barrel of love.

Kenneth and Wayne

No one in Homerville could remember the last time Kenneth and Wayne had spoken to each other. The older wags allowed as how the Portwood brothers ignored each other's presence as far back as their high school days. Kenneth was a bit taller and thus became the basketball team's center. Wayne played forward and wouldn't pass to him, no matter if the score was tied, five seconds hung on the clock, and Kenneth was wide open.

Coach Reel was frustrated, he was puzzled, and he was as close as he ever came to becoming angry, but how could you take your two highest scorers out of the game? Individually they were all-stars. Together, frustrating.

The Portwoods were raised west of Homerville on a farm James Eldon Portwood had inherited from his father-in-law. It was a square 640 acres that laid flat and had plenty of water that James Eldon considered pretty much a waste since he farmed only grain and had little use for livestock … except for a couple of 4-H heifers that he kept for his boys.

"The boys don't need to talk as long as they do their work," he'd tell anyone who would inquire as to his sons' complete silence toward one another. "Too much talkin' in the world as it is. Me and Margaret got the quietest house in the county." And it was. James Eldon thought his boys' silence toward one another was unusual but nothing to worry about. Margaret thought it was just plain weird and had always supposed that since both boys were products of difficult and prolonged labor, they had probably been damaged somewhere in the birth canal.

When James Eldon was crushed to death by his Ford 8N while mowing a levee, Margaret moved into town to live with her sister. The boys were 20 and 21 and no longer in much need of a woman around the house. "Besides," she said, "I don't know what the hell's wrong with 'em. I can't stand the silence."

And so there they lived, both remaining bachelors until their death. Harold Bright, their second cousin, said that they conducted business by notes written on scraps of newspaper and left on the table.

"Gone to Lawrence's Implement. Looking for a John Deere." Signed simply, "Kenneth."

Then the following day Wayne would find the bill for the new tractor on the kitchen table, he'd write a check for his half, and the deal was complete.

Kenneth cooked most meals, ate his fill, then went out on the back porch to smoke. Wayne would hear the door slam, come into the kitchen and eat his dinner, then wash the dishes. Kenneth would get the mail every afternoon and leave Wayne's letters on the table. Wayne would clean the house every Sunday morning while Kenneth was attending the Presbyterian Church. Wayne attended Saturday night services with the Methodists. Kenneth did the washing and Wayne ironed their clothing.

Mrs. Portwood would come out once a month to check on things. She'd sit out on the porch and chat with Kenneth then step into the living room to see Wayne. She'd see the boys in town nearly every day, and they were both good about visiting their mother … separately … but Margaret continued her visits since this was her chance to carry messages back and forth between her sons. Kenneth had planned to start planting the next day and he needed Wayne to run the seed wagon. Wayne needed help moving the combine across the creek so Margaret asked Kenneth if he'd be sure to go pick him up. One Sunday afternoon she relayed the news that Wayne was missing a work shirt and could Kenneth please look in his closet to see if he had it. The boys' silence seemed a polite and civilized standoff.

As far as anyone could tell, the only semi-tragedy that ever came from their sixty years of living without speaking was the pile of rotten corn. The Portwood brothers kept the neatest farm in the township. Twice their homestead had been featured on the cover of farm magazines. This made the ten-foot pile of rotting corn in their driveway even more of a puzzling eyesore.

It was sometime in the early seventies. Wayne was dumping a load of corn into an auger and Kenneth was standing near the rear of the truck, moving the tailgate up and down to regulate the flow. Of course, the rest of this is pure neighbor speculation since there were no other witnesses and the brothers themselves never spoke of it. Charlie Walker said he drove by and the truck's grain bed had become unbalanced and flipped backwards, leaving poor Kenneth standing there covered in shelled corn with the yellow grain cascading over the tailgate. This sort of mishap was not totally uncommon, and the cure was to start scooping the grain into the hopper by hand. But as near as anyone could tell, neither of the Portwood boys felt they were to blame for the 200-bushel splotch of shelled corn besmirching their otherwise pristine homestead. The corn stayed there until winter … then through the spring … and through the next summer. The once yellow mountain of grain turned brown when the snows hit, then black and fungus-encrusted as the weather warmed in June. And still the mound would not be moved. Kenneth and Wayne had driven around the pile so long that their driveway now had a permanent curve, and the smell emitted by this moldy mass could only be recognized by farmers old enough to remember corn mash liquor. The locals called it Mount Portwood.

Elmer Lawrence, a neighbor whose sense of propriety and neatness exceeded even the Portwood boys, finally loaded up his boys one July afternoon when he knew that Kenneth and Wayne were out haying, scooped the musty mess into his truck and hauled it off.

Ronnie Logsdon now owns the Portwood place and says he still has to cut the volunteer corn out of his driveway every summer.

Kenneth and Wayne's eccentric ways became as much a part of the local landscape as McKee Creek and the black, rich dirt that surrounded Homerville. Only on one dangerous occasion did their unconventional behavior cause what could have called public notice. By this time the brothers barely acknowledged each other's existence, much less his presence.

Their mother Margaret's clogged birth canal theory had proven to be at least in part correct. Both boys were neat, both were hard working, and both shared a sort of lunacy. Wayne would tip his head to the left when he spoke to you and his conversation was peppered with short bursts of "Oh, well," and "Yes, that's maybe just about it," and "What? Oh, yes. Well." Kenneth, as might be expected, also talked with a tilted head, but his tipped significantly to the right, and he had a curious and sometimes maddening blink when excited. He'd also grunt a great deal for reasons known only to him and God.

Their Uncle Hershel died in Indiana, and Cousin Harold Bright was put in charge of the estate. Some few thousand dollars were due the Portwood boys, so it was Harold's job to meet with them together. After the strange interview, Harold dashed back to town to report the most unique three-way conversation of his lifetime.

Harold began, "So I suppose you know Uncle Hershel died?" Kenneth sat out on the porch and Wayne at the kitchen table. Harold positioned himself in a straight-back chair, sitting squarely in the doorway between them. "He left us all a little money."

"Yes, well," said Wayne. "I guess that would be about right."

"There's about four thousand for each of you boys."

Kenneth began blinking. "That's very kind of you, Harold."

"Oh, it isn't me," chuckled Harold.

Kenneth began a emitting a low grunt much like a sow halfway through the birth of a dozen piglets. Harold looked at him but Kenneth seemed unaware of his own grunting.

"Yes, well," said Wayne. "I guess that would be about right."

Harold continued. Wayne smoked. Kenneth began blinking and grunting simultaneously and in a sort of aboriginal rhythm.

"There are papers to sign, of course," said Harold.

"What? Oh, yes. Well." said Wayne.

"I'll need both your signatures."

"Both?" said Kenneth.

"Who else?" said Wayne.

"Both of you. You Wayne, and Kenneth of course."

Harold said that this was the strangest part of the afternoon's already loony conversation. Both brothers looked at him as if it was Harold who was loony. Neither seemed aware of having a brother.

"It's for the lawyers, you know. Both signatures. It's easy, really. If you'll both just …"

"Both?" said Kenneth, not in an angry nor territorial way but simply confounded that Harold would speak of a brother who did not exist. Although Harold was bewildered by the logic of it all, he quickly realized what was happening.

"Here, Kenneth," he said. "You sign here." Kenneth signed. Then he walked inside to the kitchen table and said, "Wayne, this is where you sign." He made no further mention of the other brother. Harold simply handed them each an envelope with a check, tipped his hat, and made his way to the car wondering who Kenneth thought was washing his dishes every morning.

It was this mild form of lunacy that put the incident of '51 in perspective. Apparently Kenneth briefly came to his senses one morning and realized, at least for a moment, that his brother existed. In fact, for some reason he discovered that his brother was a bit loopy. Wayne had washed the windows on a particularly sub-zero day in January and the water had frozen to all the panes. Kenneth decided that his brother needed to be locked up.

Kenneth crept into the living room, picked up the phone, and called the sheriff, stating that his name was Kenneth Portwood, he lived two miles west of Homerville on the Baylis gravel road, and that his brother had gone mad and was in need of locking up. When asked why he thought this, Kenneth replied that his brother was washing windows in mid-winter.

The dispatcher said, "Is that all he's doing?"

Noting a disturbing bit of doubt in the officer's mind, Kenneth added, "And he's threatened to kill me. He aimed his shotgun at me while I was bathing this morning and fired. I think he may have also killed our father. I can't find him."

Kenneth made up this last bit for insurance. Of course, the item about not being able to find his father was true, James Eldon Portwood already being some thirty years dead.

Kenneth's plan to have Wayne committed would have worked well had not Wayne overheard the conversation while shining his shoes in the next room. It was Sunday morning and he always shined his shoes in the kitchen on Sunday morning. At first he wondered who could be on the phone, then something clicked a trigger in his memory and he not only remembered that he had a brother living in the same house, but that same brother was trying to have him sent away to an asylum. His hands were already frozen from washing windows, but he slipped on his gloves and boots then walked out to the end of the driveway to wait for the sheriff.

The Portwoods seldom traveled further than Homerville to do their trading, so when the sheriff arrived at their farm, he had no idea he was talking to Wayne instead of Kenneth.

"He's right up there in the house, Sheriff," said Wayne.

"You think he's dangerous? Got a gun or anything?"

"I locked up the shotgun. He'll be getting dressed for church right now. You'll find him in the first bedroom on your right."

"You say he tried to kill you?"

"Yes. And on a Sunday. He's crazy, sir."

"You stay put and I'll call for some help," said the sheriff.

"And by the way," said Wayne. "He'll claim he's me. He'll say you have the wrong man, but he's always doing that. Been loony since birth, sad to say."

"We'll take care of him. And your name again ... for the report?"

"Kenneth Portwood," said Wayne.

"You just stay put. These things happen and it's best you let me take care of it."

"Yes, well," said Wayne. "I guess that would be about right."

When the deputy arrived and they led Kenneth handcuffed out of the house, he was not violent, but as Wayne had predicted, he did protest that they had the wrong man.

Kenneth eventually came home after a few days of evaluation and complete confusion on the part of both the Mental Health Services Department and the sheriff. Mrs. Portwood was eventually located and she identified the proper child but by that time the sheriff and the Mental Health Services Department simply wanted to be rid of the case. No one seemed violent, Mrs. Portwood seemed merely vexed, and Kenneth and Wayne were deemed a bit loony but generally harmless.

How the Portwood boys spent their days and indeed their lives was the cause of much speculation and entertainment in Homerville. What if Wayne were injured? Would Kenneth go for help? What if one of the brothers died? Would he simply lie there for weeks until someone thought to check? And of course the most frustrating question of the lot: Why didn't they speak? What had caused all this? Margaret Portwood claimed she didn't know, and in fact for the last thirty years she hadn't even wondered. She said the boys were in 7th and 8th grade when it happened and for that matter, she didn't think she even knew the cause at the time. One day at breakfast they chose not to speak to each other and for some sixty years they kept it up.

When their father had died, the two boys along with four nephews carried him to the grave. The minister was new to town and didn't know the boys' history. He came to the house on the night of his death and asked if he could speak to them together.

Wayne said, "No."

Kenneth replied, "Who?"

If truth were known, plenty of folks had the opportunity to tell the young minister about the Portwood brothers' peculiarities but they wanted to see what happened if left on his own.

"Perhaps I should start again," said the minister. Wayne was on the porch smoking. Kenneth was sitting at the kitchen table. "If perhaps you could come out on the porch to join your brother …"

"Who?" asked Kenneth.

"Your brother. He's on the porch. I'm speaking to him right now."

Kenneth began blinking in rhythm to the Seth Thomas clock hanging above the stove. Then he began grunting a sort of counterpoint to the ticking. The young preacher took this as some sort of rural prelude to an act of extreme violence and took his leave immediately, shouting at Wayne as he jumped from the porch, "See you at the funeral!"

"Yes, well," said Wayne. "I guess that would be about right."

Kenneth died first. Wayne awoke one morning and found that his breakfast was not ready. He looked outside and Kenneth's truck was still parked in the garage, then he looked into his brother's bedroom and saw him lying dead on the floor. Wayne called the undertaker then fixed his own breakfast.

Numerous stories sprung up around the events of the funeral. Iris Little swore she saw a tear running down Wayne's face during the final prayer. Myrna Peele swore that Margaret had to talk Wayne into attending at all. One thing was sure … all eyes were on Wayne during the service, the whole town curious as to the silent brother's reaction.

Another couple of winters and Wayne was gone as well. Margaret Portwood, still lucid and lively at 94, saw her husband and both sons buried. She inherited back the farm that should have been hers in the first place, then promptly gave most of it to her nephew, Harold Bright, and with the inheritance he set up a little bookstore on Main Street. Thanks to the Portwood brothers, the residents of Homerville can purchase a volume of Zane Gray or Faulkner then go home and read … in silence.

The Rise and Fall of Daisy Miller

Harold Bright rose that Christmas morning, washed under his arms and put on a white shirt with a red sweater vest, which was about as festive as Harold ever got.

Harold generally avoided social events but this after all was December 25th. He had only one nephew and that nephew's wife insisted that he join them for Thanksgiving, Easter, and Christmas. She assumed since he was a bachelor that he led a singularly lonely life. Although Harold Bright sniffed at such a supposition, he attended the holiday dinners, sat patiently while his nephew and wife asked inane questions of their children, and carried on a constant monologue with each new paragraph beginning with, "And tell Uncle Harold how you …" "Tell Uncle Harold about …" and "I'll be bet Uncle Harold didn't know that you …"

This is all so … well … bosh, Harold would think to himself. So terribly bosh.

Harold loved the word. Bosh. He'd read it in a Henry James novel and anything he ever found in a Henry James novel he immediately deemed wonderful and well said. In fact, when the world pushed Harold into a tedious corner, say a Christmas dinner, his mind would race off to embrace the characters he'd met in Henry James novels. His nephew became Peter Quint in *The Turn of the Screw*, and his nephew's wife would take on the ghostly appearance of the governess, Mrs. Jessel. His nephew's children would blather on about spelling competitions and honor rolls while Harold imagined them to be the two children, Flora and Miles. These literary imaginings saved Harold from the discomfort of enduring gatherings and it made him wish all the more that he could soon return to his bookshop.

Bright's Books was located in the telephone office once occupied by Alice Holeman, then the building later served as the post office before Margaret Hoerlein built the new post office just west of there. Harold Bright sold books mainly as a pretense for running a bookstore. He said that he specialized in rare books, thus explaining to the town why none of us had ever heard of many of the volumes he collected.

On this Christmas morning he sat diligently at his nephew's dinner table, checking his watch and wondering how long before he could politely make excuses and get back to his store. His little niece was telling him how much fun she'd had as a candy cane in a local ballet production of the *Nutcracker* while Harold smiled politely and wondered about the need for children at all. Oh, he knew the anthropological requirements of sustaining the race and was fairly well schooled on the biology of the process, but as to the actual raising, feeding, bedding, dressing, petting, powdering, diapering, schooling, and orthodontic requirements, he wondered if it wouldn't be less bothersome to simply put them away somewhere until they were old enough to enjoy fine books. He smiled at Jessie and said that, "Yes, I'd love to come watch your performance next year. Please remind me when it's coming up, won't you?" She giggled that she most certainly would while Harold Bright eyed his wristwatch. Another five minutes and he'd fulfill his social quota of minutes for the season.

"What about dessert, Uncle Harold?" His nephew's wife made a Chocolate Hazelnut Torte every Christmas since it was an old Irish tradition handed down the Bright family line for generations. Harold knew perfectly well that Chocolate Hazelnut Tortes were neither a Bright tradition nor were they Irish. Tortes were as Austrian as the Brights were English, and Henry James would tell you all this in a minute, but Harold said, "Charlotte, your torte is one of the highlights of my Christmas season!" and despite his flirtation with diabetes, he'd allow himself one holiday indulgence and eat her torte.

It takes exactly three minutes and fifteen seconds to eat a large slice of Chocolate Hazelnut Torte, which brought Harold precisely to the time of his planned departure for the store.

"Oh! So soon, Uncle Harold? We hardly ever get to see you!"

"So many things to do before tomorrow," he'd say.

"Please … another torte? It's Christmas!" Charlotte would often send food home with Harold on these holiday excursions. Harold would let the food sit in his tiny refrigerator for a respectful amount of time, then toss it out. Whether consuming books or leftover turkey, Harold preferred making his own choices.

"Just another cup of coffee?"

"Oh, heavens, I'm swimming now!" he'd laugh as he grabbed his scarf from the stairway. "Such a delight seeing all of you again," said Harold Bright. "I can't tell you how much I appreciate being with you at Christmas," said Harold Bright. "Merry Christmas!" he chuckled, and he was gone.

Harold Bright was a little fellow, pleasantly rounded on the edges, his bald head neatly framed by a half-halo of coal black hair which he kept smartly trimmed. He was clean-shaven except for a small brush of a moustache with which he constantly twiddled when he read. He never went out in the wintertime without his large woolen top coat, a full-length muffler wrapped a dozen times around his neck and chin, and all topped off with what we called a lumberjack hat, red and white checks with large earmuffs that hung down to his shoulders. Once Harold got dressed for the outdoors, there was very little of him left showing. He'd hurry to his car as if he'd have something important to do, run the two stop signs on Main Street as if he was in a hurry, then dash into the store as if the world depended on him opening up every morning. Which it never did.

Bright's Books was not the sort of place that would draw you in. One long, dark room with bookshelves to nearly the 12-foot ceiling ... Harold bought them from Reel Brothers when they remodeled and was so anxious to fill them with books that he didn't even screw them to the walls … just placed them along each side and let the very weight of his volumes hold them in place … long counters left over from the telephone days, two black ceiling fans covered with the oil and dust of a half-century's neglect, and a smell of must and leather that reminded you of old horses. It was Harold's kind of place. An attractive and welcoming store would have attracted too many visitors and it was Harold Bright's full intention to live on his inheritance, collect a monthly check from the government, and read his books unmolested.

Harold waved one last time as his nephew's family gathered on their front porch to see him off. "Just a lovely old man, Jim. I just wish we could do more for him. Seems so very lonely."

"He does?" Jim had never thought of his Uncle Harold as lonely. Eccentric perhaps, and maybe a bit more brilliant than most, but he seemed happy enough with his lot.

"Oh, yes," said Charlotte. "Can't you see it in his eyes?"

"Well, I suppose so. If you say so."

"We should have him over more often."

"I'm not sure that …"

"Oh, of course we will. You can tell he loves it when he's around our children."

"Well, I suppose so. If you say so."

"Oh, my. I forgot to wrap up some leftovers. I always send something home with Harold."

"He seemed … well, yes, I suppose … I don't know if …"

Harold's heart beat a little faster as he approached his store. The darkness of a winter's afternoon was approaching and he'd been away for … what? … nearly four hours now. No telling what had transpired since he left early that morning. He noticed that none of the other stores in Homerville were open on Christmas. Such a shame, he thought, that the other businessmen didn't love their work as he did.

He jammed the old iron key into the lock and after the usual wrangling it kicked the tumbler free. Harold opened the door and breathed deeply of the must and leather and lingering sweetness of the coal oil fumes. Home again, he thought. 'Tis so sweet to be home again. He shut the door and toyed with the idea of turning the laminated "Closed" sign to "Open," then thought … no … if anyone wants anything they can see my car. Besides, some of the local church wags might think poorly of him for opening on Christ's birthday. He wasn't against religion, he just found it so … well, unimaginative. He very much admired the language of the King James Bible but there was never any talk of ghosts, of beautiful Englishwomen touring the continent, of smoky Parisian bars or goblins masquerading as serving maids. So … well, so bosh.

The little man bathed a moment in the warmth of his little stove then grabbed the counter to steady himself. Too much sugar, he thought. Why do people do these things? Or perhaps it was the sudden warmth that made him dizzy.

Harold tossed his layers of wraps onto the counter and headed quickly for his lair, a cozy nest of a reading spot he'd created at the far back of his store. You would have thought that a man who spent his nose in books might favor a comfortable recliner or perhaps a couch to spend his hours, but to Harold, reading was a business … a serious business that required a serious chair. His particular throne was an oak swivel he'd purchased from the Wayne Feeds store when Homer Berry got out of the business. It slid neatly into the table where Alice Holeman once kept her telephone operator's apparatus. This was how a man was supposed to read … feet on the floor, hard-backed chair, and a simple table. He'd added a small, checkered cushion last August as a concession to his hemorrhoids, but other than that, it was a Spartan experience.

Harold knew what he was to read that evening. In fact, he'd thought of little else since he got out of bed that morning and his yearnings for the book were all that sustained him through Charlotte's baked ham and cheese potatoes. He imagined holding the book while Jim talked of investments and dance lessons, and by the time the mislabeled torte was served, he could almost read the opening lines. He reached out and took hold of *The Portrait of a Lady*, by Henry James. James had started to write this novel in Florence in 1879 then moved to Venice where he continued writing while living on the Riva Sciavoni near the passage leading off to San Zaccaria. How could one think of Irish/Austrian tortes when dreaming of the Italian waterfront spread out before him so sumptuously? Bosh. So absolutely bosh.

This must have been … what? … his sixth reading of the book, or perhaps the seventh? But with James, unlike so many authors, each reading brought a new insight, a new appreciation for the master's skill with words and nuance. This was his Christmas dessert, a present to himself far more grand than anything a doting niece might lay in his lap. And when I finish this, he thought … but no! … I must not get ahead of myself … one thing at a time … no room for gluttony here … but yes, when I finish this, then it's *Daisy Miller*. What a splendid way to start the new year … *Daisy Miller!* I know just where I put James' little queen … second section on the east, top shelf … the very top shelf. Harold hadn't visited the top shelf for years. After all, there was so much wonder at his feet, but next … next would be top shelf *Daisy Miller!*

He fingered the spine on *Portrait of a Lady*. He lifted her in his right hand and judged her weight. As a book should be, he thought. Heft. It's heft that makes a book. You can't pick up a moving picture like this, he thought. You can't bounce a painting up and down in your hand. This is a book! This is … this is life itself!

Harold's mind often ran to the tragic and already he envisioned the sadness with which he'd have to leave his book tonight to drive the two blocks to home and bed. And then tomorrow … oh, bother, tomorrow he'd have to go next door to get the mail … that would be an interruption … No, he'd take the book with him, read it on the way. But what would people think? Only twenty-seven steps to the post office and he takes a book? … then lunch, then a nap. And what if someone were to come in to buy a book? Oh bosh! he thought. I'll stay closed just one more day. I'll read all night then most of tomorrow and by closing time I'll be ready to climb up and get Daisy and …

The thoughts were too, too heady for Harold. He gazed toward the front of the store and saw the first snowflakes silhouetted against the streetlight. One cup of tea and he'd be set for the evening. He, the tea, and Henry. He pitied anyone tonight who was stuck in the midst of family, friends and Christmas. They'll never know, thought Harold. They'll just never know.

Harold pulled the desk drawer out against his belly and searched for his steel mesh pincher spoon. He carefully filled it with the small, crushed tealeaves from the stone pot near his reading lamp then put the kettle to boil. Alice Holeman had kept a burner plate for this very purpose and Harold always took some pride in the fact that the hotplate had never been used for anything but making tea. Henry James would have smiled. Harold was one of the few men in Central Illinois who could listen to a boiling kettle of water and know exactly when the temperature had reached 212 degrees and he knew that two and one half minutes of steeping made the perfect sip. Three minutes and you'd be drinking a bitter cup. Steeping tea, he thought … who out there in their little houses with their little children and their little thoughts and little dreams would right at this moment experience a pleasure anything like steeping the perfect cup of tea? Indeed. Bosh indeed.

Harold Bright carefully lifted the mesh spoon out of the cup, he raised the cup to his lips, closed his eyes and inhaled deeply of the aroma of Five Roses tea. Harold smiled. Gone were thoughts of business, of ceremony, of social necessities, of proctologists and beauty pageants, ballet lessons and tortes. His right hand holding the cup of Five Roses and his left about to open to the preface of Portrait of a Lady, let the others describe their heavens full of noisy-winged angels and trumpet-tooting seraphim's, this was his paradise. His ecstasy was here on an oak swivel chair under the soft glow of a reading lamp. He poised his lips to drink … and the knocking began.

The best and worst of times crashed in upon Harold simultaneously as the seductive aroma of Five Roses filled his nostrils and the knocking became more persistent. The tea had already dropped to 164 degrees in the steeping process, another six degrees while he'd so foolishly wasted his time basking in the aroma, and by the time he got up to answer the door and returned … even with the briefest conversation with the intruder and the most hurried shuffle down the length of the store, the temperature would be down to at least 100 degrees and unfit for anything but spitting holes in the snow. Bosh! Damn it to hell and bosh!

He glanced toward the door and saw a small, stocking-capped figure with her nose pressed against the glass. He'd been seen and could not ignore the miscreant's pounding. He'd have to answer the door, boil the water again, steep the tea … all amounting to the first chapter of his night's longing. Bosh! Damn it to hell and bosh!

He slammed the cup down onto his reading table, pushed the swivel back against a row of bookshelves, and steamed toward door, doing his best imitation of a surgeon interrupted in the middle of a lobotomy. When he got to the door, he recognized the face. Jim's girl Jessie. He opened the door.

"What a delightful surprise! Jenny!"

"Jessie. I have something for you, Uncle Harold!"

From behind her back she produced a small mound of tinfoil.

"It's mommy's Chocolate Hazelnut Torte. We knew you liked it so we brought you what we had left."

Harold looked out into the snow. Jim, Charlotte and the boy whose name he could not recall were pressed against the windshield, waving their mittens.

"Merry Christmas, Uncle Harold!" and Jessie was running down the concrete steps and back to the waiting car. Jim honked and Harold waved, smiling broadly as the snowflakes hit his cheeks. The car backed into the street and honked again as his nephew's family waved. Harold returned the wave and with it an even bigger smile designed to be seen at a greater distance. Harold backed into the store, locked the door, and shouted, "Damn! Bosh fritters damn and Creole-nation!"

The evening was shot. Ten minutes until nine and Harold could never stay awake past ten thirty. Another fifteen minutes to make tea, then read a few chapters, drive home, take a bath and crawl into bed. It couldn't be done. Not tonight. The evening was ruined beyond repair. To think, he thought, that this was what I lived for today. To think, he thought, what I endured just to savor this few brief moments. To think … to think! Something had to be salvaged. Days are not to be wasted like this … not even Christmas day. There must be something he could do to throw his conscience a bone of meaning, something to salvage and then say, "Yes, well done. Good job, Harold. Now let's call it day." But what?

Harold looked down the darkened alleyway of Bright's Books … a shadowy canyon of Bunyon and Faulkner and Poe and Hawthorne. Long, dusty volumes of Joyce, Emerson, Balzac, and Thoreau stared down at him, daring him he imagined, to take them up and salvage something of the final minutes. Dear God, an evening with Henry James blown away like a single tealeaf in a dullard's breeze of Chocolate Hazelnut torte. Something … something … what? Catalog a few wayward volumes … too much time needed … jot a few musings in his journal about James' tendencies toward the supernatural … no, too mind consuming this late at night … something … something to be salvaged, but what? His eyes raced across the dusty shelves … Cervantes, Bunyon, Defoe, Swift, Fielding … what? what? … something to make this evening worth his breathing it … look up … up further … and … yes.

The next book. The one he'd promised himself for the new year. Harold had hired the Turner boys to stack the shelves when he moved into the store, but he knew the location of every volume. *Daisy Miller*. Somewhere up there, just to the left of the tar-patched crack in the pressed tin ceiling … just there above the Dickens collection … that's where he had the boys put *Daisy Miller*.

Harold Bright nearly danced to the back of the store and grabbed the rolling ladder. Tonight he'd at least find *Daisy Miller* and bring her down to reading level … he'd at least accomplish this. The old ladder clanged along on the ancient roller track, catching a bit on each coupling, Harold giving the ladder a quick jerk and freeing it to roll down the rail. There … that should just about … yes … the ladder was directly in line with Daisy, and Harold Bright began to climb.

Vertigo had never been a problem for Harold but blood pressure was always a concern. He stopped a moment on the third rung to steady himself. The shadows swayed but it must be … it must be the wind blowing the light bulb … just a few more steps and … "It was that damned torte," he said to himself. "Or the ham. That's pork isn't it? You can undercook pork." But Harold Bright wasn't sick … he was dizzy. No matter, he thought … a few more steps, grab Daisy and back down we … we … Did I hear the door open? That couldn't … I mean the door is locked … and the shadows … where in the hell was the wind coming from? Then he said it aloud. He nearly screamed it. "Bosh and feather! Bosh it all! Climb old boy! Your prize awaits you and …" But the room no longer swayed, it shook. It spun. It whirled and dove and gasped. Harold Bright grabbed for the bookshelf as his ladder swung out from under his feet. He grabbed for the bookshelf and the bookshelf grabbed him back.

He'd been in a terrible hurry to set up shop and Sherm Turner told him, "Mr. Bright, we oughta nail down these shelves, you know. They're tippy when you get to the top of 'em." And yes, yes, yes, he meant to do that once he got himself settled in, but, "Yes! Of course we must. But just stack them for now, won't you? Just stack them and be careful." And Sherm was as careful as Harold was not. Harold grabbed at the shelf to steady himself and the tall maple monster leaned out from the wall … some four hundred books, seven rows of heavy volumes, each gaining momentum as the bookcase leaned even further into the room. The ladder was now resting against the west wall and Harold's fingers dug deeply into the years and years of varnish and dust as the entire case, including Harold, came crashing to the floor.

In his last remaining hours on earth Harold lay there surrounded … one could say consumed … by the books he loved so much. And there, just within grasp of his right hand lay *Daisy Miller*. This is indeed one stroke of luck, thought Harold. He would sit here and read his beloved Daisy until someone came along. Then he saw a small problem. When he grabbed the book it was open to page one. Harold had only his right hand unpinned and so he could read only that page. He could, of course, take the chance of flipping the book in the air, hoping the pages would turn a bit and he could then continue on page two, but chance-taking wasn't … ladders and bookcases aside … a part of Harold's nature. He was too much afraid of losing the book altogether in the pile of wood and paper that now blocked the store's aisle. So he read page one of *Daisy Miller*, then he read it again. And again. Sometime long after his 10 p.m. bedtime, Harold Bright fell asleep and the book dropped from his grasp.

One of the little imagined disadvantages of running a rare bookstore in a small town is the fact that it can be weeks before a customer walks in. Even a customer entering his shop on the morning following Harold's crash might have found him in time to save his life. But no one did. The sign said "Closed" and in Homerville we pay attention to the written word.

The Hotel

Ma Runkel would fix the same breakfast every morning. Six strips of bacon, eggs fried in the bacon grease, two chunks of toast roasted just short of burnt, and orange juice. On Sundays she'd fix French Toast but she couldn't remember for sure how to make French Toast so she often pretended it was Saturday instead.

Ma would carefully put his breakfast on a tin tray bordered with the colors of the Swedish flag, then climb the fourteen steps to the second story of the hotel where she'd leave her son's food in front of his door. He'd tend to eat in bits. Sometimes she'd go up to fetch the tray before noon and the food was only half gone, but if she'd wait until nearly supper the platter would be clean. He never wanted lunch, just breakfast and supper so that's what she served him.

It seemed an odd eating pattern but the rats loved it. Gary Runkel had been dead for seventeen years so the rodents didn't dare remind Ma of this or they'd be forced into the workaday life of the outdoor rats and be obliged to find their own breakfast. They secretly wished she wouldn't have burnt the toast quite so badly but to a rat it's any port in a storm.

The Homerville Hotel had only three residents by this time: Ma Runkel, Lap Toosman who was too drunk to find his room and thus stayed in various beds from night to night, and Ma's son Gary who was dead. Fact is, Gary was in the Homerville cemetery next to his father (also dead), but Ma never quite accepted the fact and fixing his meals gave her a purpose in life. That and the pinball machine.

The Homerville Hotel had the last remaining commercial, semi-mechanical pinball machine in Central Illinois. American Vending Sales in Oak Grove had made Ma countless offers to buy the thing back to put on display but Ma saw no reason to give up her sole source of income. And besides that, William Jennings Bryan had once played the machine. This was probably not true. William Jennings Bryan did marry a girl from Homerville and he did stay overnight at the hotel. Darby Sitton claimed to own the pen with which he wrote love notes to the future Mrs. Bryan. Trouble was, this machine was electric and electric pinball machines didn't exist until 1933. This would have made Bryan 93 if he'd played the machine the year it came out. Since he died at 65 this made the historic game a fact that Homerville chose to ignore. We assumed that if Gary Runkel could eat burnt toast 17 years after his death, then maybe old W.J.B. could still flip his flipper several years after his own demise.

The hotel was built sometime around the turn of the century, but, like most buildings in Homerville, the date of its birth had been long lost. Thirty-three rooms, two fairly large banquet areas each with a fireplace, and a lobby housing Ma Runkel's desk, a key rack with no keys, and the pinball machine. The place thrived in the days of muddy roads and traveling salesmen but a series of four different owners had given up on the place and Ma Runkel bought it for a song … and for Gary. The cause of her dementia was plain. Gary died in Korea and she went nuts. Her insanity was as swift as it was silent. One day she was fine, cleaning rooms, greeting guests, and being a wonderfully wholesome part of the community and the next day she received the news of her son's death and quietly went off her nut.

It started with the walking. She'd walk anywhere and everywhere and all the time. The fourth and last time the Reel Brothers' General Store was robbed, Carl and Riley entered the front door at two in the morning, 12-gauge shotguns loaded and cocked, while brother Hank waited out back just west of the loading dock. When the two burglars came running out the back door Hank shouted, "Halt." They didn't and he plugged one in the air while the other got away … at least as far as Jacksonville. Hank had done this three times before but he'd never actually killed anyone. He said he was waiting there, crouched behind the Kent Feeds sign when the most astounding thing happened. Ma Runkel came walking right through the gunfire. He said she never wavered when his gun went off … just kept on walking, practically underneath the feet of the flying intruder. He told the police that he'd have shot both men but was afraid of hitting Ma.

When the state police questioned Ma the next morning she simply said, "I don't know what the hell you're talking about," and shut the door in their faces. They knew Ma, at least by reputation, and didn't take the matter any further. Things like that happened in the days before counseling and brain medicine. After Ma's fourth moving violation the cops had come to forcibly take her license, and when they opened her door they saw the license laying on her desk and Ma sitting there with a loaded shotgun in her lap. She smiled and said, "There it is. You want it, take it." They thanked her for her time and backed out the same way they came in.

Ma would read the Bible every night … aloud and loudly. Sometimes she'd sit out on her front stoop and hold forth from the books of Revelation or Chronicles … never anything very interesting, but no one had the gumption to complain about the scriptures being read, even at top volume. She often took her own supper with her parents who'd moved to town after a long life on the farm. Her mother Maude was about the meanest woman who ever ran somebody off a road. You'd have to look long and hard to find anything good about Maude and even after a wide search you'd like as not come up empty-handed. She drove her husband Fred to deafness. It's a fact. The doctors could find nothing physically wrong with Fred's ears, but he couldn't hear a thing. We all knew the reason … Fred just got tired of listening.

One day while returning from a trip to the doctor in Riverview, Fred and Maude were both killed in a car crash. The weather was fine, the road was dry, and Oscar Harris could find no sign of heart problem in Fred's body at the mortuary. They'd just crossed the bridge and were heading down a long stretch of bottom farmland where the trees had all been cleared off fifty years ago to produce some of Illinois' finest farm ground. That is, except for one oak. Distances on the river bottom were measured from that one remaining tree. That's the one Fred hit. There were no witnesses. A five-mile stretch of open road and only one tree and Fred simply ran off the road and put the oak between him and Maude. We figured that he'd just gotten tired of listening.

The hotel was located on the south side of Main Street, across from Hap Lyman's lumber yard which stood just across the alley from Darby Sitton's store. Aside from the salesman and an occasional itinerant preacher, the old hotel also housed several single ladies who taught at Homerville High. They ranged from the rigid and formidable Elsie Hill who could stare down a 200 pound senior farm boy with a single, deadly glare, to Judy Roseville whose little apartment was frequented by far too many Homerville high school boys. She called it her "Literary Club," and it was a safe place to go smoke without getting caught. Some said worse of Miss Roseville, but none of the boys ever confessed anything more than getting a bit hot and bothered by Miss Roseville's rendition of the Rubayat of Khayyam.

Ah Love! could you and I with Him conspire
To grasp this sorry Scheme of Things entire,
Would not we shatter it to bits-and then
Re-mould it nearer to the Heart's Desire!

When Arlene Scranton found this scribbled on her young Burt's notebook, she took him to the Methodist minister who deemed the scribblings to be not only harmless, but in fact, of some literary merit. Arlene, her husband, seven sons, and one daughter soon became the newest members of the Presbyterian Church. This doubled the church's weekly attendance and they had Judy Roseville to thank.

Perhaps the most interesting inhabitant of the Homerville Hotel was Dr. Engel's daughter Heidi. Heidi was the only child of Frau Engel and Heinrich and she was born with one leg shorter than the other in an age when you just let those things go. A thin girl with almost transparent skin, Heidi was blessed with an artistic temperament and the financial means to do whatever she wanted. Dr. Engel and his wife had worked hard, lived frugally and then given all they had to Heidi in an attempt to make up for the two inches she was missing from her left leg.

When her parents had passed on, Heidi moved into a second story room on the northwest corner of the hotel facing the bandstand and most of Homerville. She could have bought the hotel instead of renting a room … fact is, she could have purchased any of Homerville that had been willing to sell, but instead the young artist (who had no special artist talent) moved into what she called her "studio room" on the second floor and would sit in her window seat on summer mornings, sipping Indian tea and making notes on a small yellow pad that she kept near the window.

Artists are more tolerated than appreciated in small towns unless they were like Hank Reel who drew "real paintings" of horses and sleighs coming home at twilight. Abstract artists were simply untalented boobs, and writers were highly suspect. You couldn't even talk to one for fear of seeing your family slandered in some novel published in St. Louis.

Although Heidi's art went several miles beyond the abstract, she was endured by most and loved by a few. When simple oddness reaches full-blown eccentricity, we can cherish it like a mis-stamped penny, and to stand out as an eccentric in a town blessed with more than its fair share of outright oddities was an accomplishment in and of itself. It was the Trash Fest that truly set Heidi apart from the everyday anomaly and established her as Homerville's queen of the genuinely abnormal.

The town's first garbage pickup service consisted of Donnie Charles's hauling our trash to the town dump. If you'd set the refuse of your teaming shore out on the curb early enough on

Friday morning (you had about a ten minute window of opportunity between Charlie's truck and Darby Sitton's dogs), Donnie would pick it up and haul it off. One Friday in the early sixties Heidi asked to ride the route with Donnie and he gladly obliged. The reason Donnie took the job was to see what other folks were throwing away. He and his wife often took slow drives around town in the evening just too see what other folks were doing. If your shades were open, they'd even stop for a bit in the street and wait for something to happen.

Heidi's mission that morning was to collect the most interesting junk from the Homerville garbage cans and build a sculpture that in her words, "… stood for all of us … who we are and who we hope to be." Although that made no sense at all to Donnie, he was glad to have the company that morning and by the time he'd made his pass down Hell Street at the end of town, Heidi had red-tagged a good deal of his load. He carefully delivered her designated junk in the alley behind the hotel and took the rest to dump.

Heidi lived in the hotel room but also kept the family home and paid Hun Masters a monthly sum to keep the grass mowed and the roof patched. It was in the Engel's slightly overgrown back yard where Hun began toting the makings of "Homerville Phoenix," the name she'd given to her work of art. I remember it was early in July because the Griggsville Fair had just ended, when we received our invitations in the mail:

Miss Heidi Engel
would be absolutely overjoyed
by the pleasure of your company
at the unveiling of "Homerville Phoenix"
Sunday afternoon at 4 p.m.
At the former residence of Dr. and Frau Engel.
Refreshments will be served.
RSVP: The Homerville Hotel Room 21

What followed that morning was a grand round of "I'll go if you will," and once Genevieve Wilson decided that she'd give it a shot, most of the town fell in line. We were met at the yard gate by Heidi dressed in something that looked suspiciously Greek and were handed a glass of Mogen David wine by Darold Toner, age 12, who'd been hired to wear a tiny kilt for the occasion. His mother said that it was a decision he'd regret for the rest of his life as he had no idea that people would bring their kids … his schoolmates … and they'd see him wearing a skirt in public.

Once we'd taken our seats on what looked a good deal like five-gallon buckets painted Sherwood Green, the trumpets began. Bradley Bartholomew, the skinny-legged first trumpet player in the Homerville Marching Heroes, stepped through an ivy-covered arch that Heidi had installed near the back door of the garage. That he was wearing a costume was a relief to Darold Toner since it took the attention off his kilt. I have no idea how much Heidi had paid Bradley to wear tights but we could tell from the look on his face that it hadn't been quite enough. He tooted an anemic fanfare then retreated quickly into the safety of the garage and his pants.

Heidi came flowing onto the grassy space in front of our buckets. Actually, with her short leg, it was a little less than a "flow," but it did somehow put us in mind of running water after a storm. It's strange how you let things get by you, but I had never noticed Heidi's ankles before that July afternoon. Delicate … like those of a dancer or one of the dainty Hummel figurines in Brant's window on the Pittsfield Square. And despite her pronounced limp, Heidi did indeed resemble a ballerina. As she spoke her hands and arms became slender reeds on the banks of the Nile, gesturing to us, to the still-draped statue about to be unveiled, and to the retreating form of Bradley Bartholomew who had now discovered that Darold Toner had stolen his pants. Those of us in the back buckets could hear Brad's muffled "Damn it to hell!" as he tore around the garage looking for his jeans.

If the measure of an artist is the bent God puts upon her soul, then Heidi was indeed an artist that day, in spite of the monstrosity she unveiled after reciting a bit of Emily Dickinson:

There came a wind like a bugle;
It quivered through the grass,
And a green chill upon the heat

So ominous did pass
We barred the windows and the doors
As from an emerald ghost;
The doom's electric moccasin
That very instant passed.
On a strange mob of panting trees
And fences fled away,
And rivers where the houses ran
The living looked that day.
The bell within the steeple wild
The flying tidings whirled
How much can come
And much can go,
And yet abide the world!

Because the assembled citizens of Homerville had no more idea than the man in the moon what either Heidi or Emily had meant by this, it seemed a fitting prelude to what was to come when Heidi reached out her right arm like the neck of a graceful swan, and pulled on the curtain cord holding the drapery in place. There was little breeze that day other than the collective sucking gasp heard from the bucketed crowd. It was … well, it was amazing. If the purpose of art is to allow the audience to experience new and theretofore unknown feelings, then the sculpture was a success already.

Rob Lackshide's boxer shorts seemed to be the focal point although this particular monument had so many points of interest that any attempt at focus soon became futile. If the work had a central theme it seemed to be discarded underthings. Wayne Orr, the only man from Homerville who ever pretended to be much of a writer, once wrote a book of short stories about his hometown, and although it was a highly fictionalized account of the Homerville citizens, most local readers missed all literary merit as they strove instead to pick out who he was talking about. Such was the case on this warm afternoon in Heinrich Engel's backyard. We had little interest in what the sculpture looked like or what it was supposed to mean but our curiosity as to what belonged to whom was verging on the rabid.

The art critics were abuzz:

"That's got to be yours."

"It most certainly is not. Look at the size of those things!"

"That's what I mean. Who else would have one that …?"

"Couldn't she at least wash 'em first?"

"That stain! Good grief, Albert, that's your stain!"

"That's where they went! You said you lost 'em!"

"I guess you don't have the biggest butt in town after all. Look at the white ones hangin' from the toaster."

After Heidi got our attention again, she told us that we were free to come up and examine her new work of art more closely. We could even touch it if we liked. We didn't, and after a few cookies and a special surprise appearance of Pastor Hammond on the autoharp, we sort of dissolved from the yard and oozed back home.

Heidi said that she wanted her art to make people think. We did. We thought a great deal that evening and the general consensus was that Heidi Engel needed to be put in a nice home somewhere … without access to paint and easel. But, like most big ideas in Homerville, this one was soon forgotten and Heidi spent the rest of her life fighting an especially horrible form of cancer that seemed to diminish her already slight frame day by day.

She made one last creative adventure when she attempted to turn the hotel into an artists' colony before her death, but that failed as her invited community of artists brought with them a type of agriculture not so much appreciated as corn and soybeans. And they tended to avoid baths.

On March 31st of 1921, a horrible fire destroyed the entire northwest section of Homerville's business district. Everyone pitched in to fight the blaze and absolutely nothing was saved. That's how it was in those days … you couldn't just let a building burn but you knew there was little hope of putting out a full-blown fire. But there was one saving grace from the fire of '21, in that the Lahr grocery store burned down. Like many rural groceries in those days, the Lahr store would buy chickens, scald and pluck them, then burn the feathers. The stench hung like an ugly sneeze over the town and you could smell the burnt feathers in your clothing years after you'd left town. After the fire there were no more chicken factories in town, but the memory of those odiferous days was fanned back to life when Heidi's community of artists moved into the hotel for one summer. It wasn't so much the smell of the artists but of the particular brand of tobacco they grew behind the store and smoked night and day. We had never known much about marijuana until that summer but all agreed that the smell was far more pleasant than burnt feathers.

Ma Runkel, not wanting to intrude on Gary's privacy, waited eighteen years before she went in to clean his room. She looked all over for the boy but it seemed as if he'd disappeared. The room was fairly tidy if you overlooked the mound of rat droppings and the chicken bones. His clothing was right where he'd left it when he went to war … a bit dusty and moth-eaten, but nothing a little soap and water wouldn't fix.

She inquired up and down Main Street if anyone had seen him recently. Some said they hadn't seen him since the Korean conflict and some claim to have talked to Gary just that morning. Made you wonder who was the looniest bird on the street. She asked if anyone could use twelve pounds of bacon since she didn't eat the stuff herself, but no one seemed to have any interest so she went back to the lobby, unplugged the pinball machine and sat down.

That's where they found her. No cause of death seemed apparent. She just sat down and didn't get up. On the site of the Homerville Hotel there's a Phillips 66 station where Billy Thele and his nephew Jake run just about the best mechanic shop in the county.

I once asked Billy if there weren't times when he worked late at night and the moon was full, if he didn't hear the clunk-clunk of Heidi coming up the stairs or the footsteps of Ma Runkel searching from room to room for Gary. Billy thought a long moment, then said, "No."

Brothers

The board of directors of Reel Brothers Groceries, Sundries and Hardware met the first Saturday of every month at 5 a.m. around the butcher's block. The meat department sat squarely at the far end of the Reel Brother's grocery room and the oak butcher's block took up a four by four section in the very center of the work area. When John Reel, Sr. bought the store in 1912, the block stood a full three feet from toe to top. By 1972 the block measured 2 feet 10 inches. Two inches in 60 years.

At the end of every meat cutting day … and that meant six days a week at Reel Brothers Groceries, Sundries and Hardware, Hank Reel would scrape down the butcher's block with his two-handed shank knife, scattering the hog and steer residue to the floor, then wash the whole block down with soapy water. And along with the fat, blood, and gristle would come a bit of the butcher's block. John Sr. had picked out the block himself in Chicago, back when the stockyards had their own supply store on the premises, and had it shipped downstate to Springfield, and then hired Charlie Wade to haul it to Homerville.

The man in Chicago said you were supposed to temper the block for a couple of days by rubbing fat into the oak surface, but John Sr. couldn't wait to start cutting meat, so he let normal wear take care of the tempering and John Sr. started selling meat.

Three sons now stood around the block for the monthly summary of where life stood in the grocery business. Hank, Riley, and Carl sipped their coffee and looked at the strips of sales receipts. Three boys, three views of their inherited grocery business. Carl was a slight man … studious, wrinkling his nose to line up his bifocals so he could read the small print. Carl knew numbers, he knew what his dad had taught him about profits, and he couldn't make a decision if his life depended on it. Riley was a bulldog … in face, in body, and in spirit. If the store was to make a good living for their three families, it would be Riley who would make it happen. Riley never met a problem he couldn't whip. The idea of defeat never crossed his mind. Hank, the tallest and oldest of the crew, was fascinated by the lines scratched across the butcher's block. They reminded him of his last trip to New Mexico where he'd spent hours looking at the drawings made by the Zuni Indians before Coronado nearly wiped them out in 1540. There were seven villages before Coronado came to town. Hank always thought that was a shame to lose so much art for just … well, for money.

Hank ran his left hand across the scratch marks. "Whatta you think, Hank?" asked Riley.

"I wonder what the Zuni's might have produced if they'd just been left alone."

"Blue jeans. We ran long again this year. You think we should cut back?"

"Folks still wear blue jeans!" smiled Carl. Carl could find a little joy even in a stack of blue jeans. Everything … absolutely everything … was fine and dandy with Carl.

"Hank, are you following me?" asked Riley. Riley loved Carl like the brother he was, but he never paid any attention to him on business matters. Everything was okay with Carl … everything in the world. He was the only brother who wore a tie to work, so it was always to Hank whom Riley would turn for an important decision.

"Folks have stopped wearing jeans like they used to," said Hank. "Maybe we oughta just sell what we've got."

"That's right," said Carl. "Things change. You never know." Carl nodded agreeably and pushed his glasses back up to the ridge of his nose.

"Did I ever show you boys the colors the Zuni's made with clay? I put some in that Lonesome Deer oil over the soup section."

Reel's store was a living art gallery of Hank's paintings, his taxidermy, and his collection of Indian pottery. "You couldn't make that color of burnt yellow if you tried. It comes from this one cave in New Mexico."

"No more jeans this year. We'll sell what we've got then see how things stand in January." Riley knew better than to spend much time talking business with Hank if Hank's mind was on the Indians, and he knew better than to ever talk business with Carl.

"Good idea," said Carl. "Real good idea. We'll see how things stand in January."

The bell over the front door tinkled. "Got customers," said Hank.

"Good day for customers. Is that about it?" asked Carl.

"That's about it," said Riley as he sighed and closed up his ledger. These monthly meetings got little accomplished, but that was fine. He made all the business decisions anyway, and if his brothers felt like they had a part by talking about blue jeans and Zuni yellow, that would have to do.

No more dissimilar business partners ever tried to make a go of a grocery store, but the Reel Brothers made it work. They'd known each other's quirks since birth and certain peculiarities had simply become a matter of course. Riley would run the business, Hank would dream, and Carl would smile a lot. There are worse things for a businessman to do than to smile a lot.

On most days you'd find Carl behind the checkout counter, manning the clangs and dings of the old brass National cash register, 25 ivory keys worn thin … 5-95 cents, No Sale, and 1-5 dollars. The bell over the door would clang, Carl would shout, "Hey! Lookee who's here!" and like as not, he'd know your name. Hank could usually be found behind the meat counter. Any male under 21 was "Young Master" to Hank. "And what would Young Master Andrews be wantin' today?" Hank had one of those faces you'd seen so many times that you completely forgot what he looked like. I can remember him being tall and balding and a bit pot bellied with a smile that erased his eyes every time he'd break into a grin. Riley was moving … forever moving. Sometimes helping carry out bags, sometimes stocking shelves, sometimes helping his brothers ring up goods or chop meat. Riley never stood still and if there was an errand to run, it was Riley's errand.

The store's office was the back of Riley's pants … a long, leather billfold stuffed with invoices and tally lists. The Reel store was laid out into three large, rectangular rooms. The center section held the groceries, the east room was home for every dry good and piece of clothing needed in the middle of Illinois, and the west room held everything else … bolts, nuts, chicken feed, woven wire, baling wire, fence posts. If you couldn't find what you wanted at Reel's store then you were simply too extravagant and that was that.

When John Reel, Sr. first opened for business, every buggy and auto in the county made his place the first stop on Saturday nights. The Homerville Community band would be torturing Sousa in the bandstand, children ran freely up and down the thick concrete sidewalks, and the stores were filled with the delight of being able to buy locally without benefit of catalog. It was John's dream to build a business large enough to support his family of three boys through thick and thin, and that's just what it did. John died while locking up one night, and the three boys worked the store until their own retirements. He'd carefully shown his sons the intricacies of buying, selling, and bartering. Riley understood all of this, Hank understood but didn't especially see the need, and Carl had no clue.

Riley's social life consisted of coming home at six, watching the news, tallying up the day's receipts and then going to bed, depending on whether the Cardinals were playing locally or on the coast. He couldn't stay up late enough to catch the coast games.

Carl's life revolved around his beloved basketball team. Not once in Homerville's history had the basketball team ever been coached by a teacher. Every coach in the school's long and often-defeated history had been a volunteer from the community. John Sr. was the town's first coach and for over thirty years, Carl became the second. As a coach, there were some better, but as a human being, Carl lead the pack. Every boy played in every game and it didn't matter if he was too fat to run, too scrawny to wrestle for the ball, or he walked with a limp. Carl believed that basketball was just about the best gift God ever gave small town America and it was his job to spread that joy around.

I was sitting behind the Homerville bench one night when Carl called time out. This was one of the few games that Homerville actually had a shot at winning and so Carl seemed to be trying especially hard tonight. He grabbed his star guard, Ken Stuabber, by the shirt front and said, "Kenny, I want you to get the ball in the middle."

Kenny looked at him and without no hint of anger said, "Damn it, Carl, we tried that and it didn't work!"

Carl thought a brief moment, said, "Well, that's fine. Let's just play ball then." And they did. And they lost. Again. If Homerville would have ever had the least chance of a winning season, I suppose that Carl might have been ousted from his coaching job, but they didn't so he wasn't. The boys all liked Carl and it didn't bother them at all to have a coach who let them do as they pleased on the basketball court. When Carl was coaching, basketball truly seemed like a game.

Hank left for Chicago after his graduation from Homerville High, and spent two years studying at the Chicago Art Institute. He was good. He was curious and bright and toward the end of his stay his professors would take him for long walks, have him over to their house for dinner, take him for coffee … each one with a different and wonderful idea of what Hank should do with his talent for perspective and his eye for line. The best offer came from a friend of a friend of a teacher who offered to pay Hank's way to France to study at Pont Aven in Brittany, a place often visited by Gauguin, Claudel, and Serusier.

Hank came back home. He said he preferred art as a pastime and was fearful that he might ruin his enjoyment of painting if he had to depend on it for a living. He always smiled when someone asked him what a talented artist was doing in a place like Homerville, and his answer was always the same. "Why not? Skies are as blue. Grass is as green. And the rent's a whole lot cheaper."

Hank was more than a painter. His carpentry still graces many homes in the town, and the home he built for himself remains one of the town's great jewels. Blue-Stucco-Gingerbread was the name he gave his particular style of architecture. The blue of the Arizona desert sky. It looked … in fact it still looks like something out of a storybook, complete with an evergreen garden and little paths cut here and there leading toward fishponds, concrete toadstools, masonry elves peeking out from behind stone walls, and a working windmill made entirely of rock found in Homer Creek. To fascinate his granddaughters he built a miniature version of his house in the garden, and inside that a miniature of the miniature house so that even the Reel dolls might have a place to play. Tucked away in one corner of the dollhouse was a tiny dollhouse for the doll's dolls.

And then there were the boats. Each winter night after supper, Hank would trounce down to the basement to work on his latest boat. All winter he'd work on the boat, in spring he'd take it apart and haul it down to his river house at Nauvoo where he'd reassemble it and ply the waves all summer. Sometime around September he'd sell the boat and come back to Homerville to build another.

I once rode with Hank in his homemade outboard skiff. He'd whip off his shirt, gun the engine and we'd be off for Keokuk or Quincy or Hannibal. Sometimes he'd sit atop his chair and steer the boat with his feet and sometimes he'd give me the wheel and I'd become Blackbeard of the Mississippi, pounding each wave with the hull as Hank would throw back his head and roar with laughter.

His river house was another wonder of our little world. After years of building things plumb and square, Hank had a new idea. This house would be improbably and completely out of whack … not a square corner in the cottage. Every door was purposely cut at an angle, the windows tilted toward the river, and even the steps to his sleeping loft tipped first to the right and then to the left as you held onto the stair rope and prayed you'd make it to the top.

Hank, being the oldest of the three brothers, did the proper thing and died first. Then, Riley who had suffered heart attacks for years, and finally Carl who was never bothered by anything much, least of all death.

Even now, some thirty years after Hank's death, his paintings are handed down from one generation of townsfolk to another, like rare Tiffany eggs or Guttenberg bibles. It's a mark of some status in Homerville to have an original Hank Reel oil hanging in your living room. Carl's ballplayers are out there … some now grandfathers … showing the world that same kindness that the old coach had shown them. Generally, they're the ones who aren't making fools of themselves by screaming at their grandchildren's referees. They know it's a game. Riley's money is somewhere … split up now I suspect … and gone.

Oscar Laughed

When Oscar Harris, the undertaker, turned eighty, he did two things of some note. He had his right leg cut off and he started smoking. He had some choice on the cigarettes but the right leg was less of an option.

"Gangrene," said Doc Denney. "It'll have to come off Oscar, or it'll poison your whole constitution."

"Well, hell," said Oscar. "I suppose so. Shoot, I'm eighty. Got fewer places to go anyway. Hack away, Doc."

The operation was safe and successful, and for the remainder of Oscar's life he sort of hopped around on one good leg, letting the stump flop where it would. He was forever trying to get Henri Strauss of Strauss Fine Clothiers, to give him a discount on one-legged suits. Being an undertaker, Oscar embalmed the leg himself, thinking that perhaps he was one of the few men on earth who'd embalmed part of his own body. He made a little box for the leg and buried it in his family plot, with a small tin sign saying, "'Til We Meet Again." He'd wanted to simply put, "See you later," but the Reverend Hammond wouldn't do the service until Oscar showed at least a small inclination toward reverence.

And that was the day he started smoking. He told his brother, my grandfather, "I've always wanted to try it. Hell, once you turn eighty what can it hurt?" Oscar smoked Old Gold filters and never did master the art of inhaling. He would lean toward the cigarette, carefully stick out his lips like he was approaching a poisonous snake, then take a drag. This is hard to do on one leg but Oscar was a remarkable man.

The undertaker in a small town was also the ambulance driver and paramedic although he never had training in anything but embalming. He'd sometimes call me late at night and say, "Wanna take a ride?" That meant that either someone had died or there had been an accident. The deaths were easier than the accidents. We'd whiz off to an accident call and Oscar would lean over to me and say, "Hope they're dead. Unless we know 'em, I mean. They're sure easier that way."

I hadn't gone on very many death runs with Uncle Oscar before I learned that fresh is better. Old man Daschel was dead nearly a week before his rural mail carrier noticed the odor, and by the time Oscar and I backed his Chevrolet hearse/station wagon up to Daschel's door, the old man had become ripe. "Why don't you just drag him out here and dump him in the well?" Oscar asked me.

"Yeh, and then I'd get all the fun. Come on, Uncle Oscar. Hold your breath and move fast."

Oscar still had two good legs on that call and we did move fast. Daschel had gone past bloat and was in lockjawed rigor when we found him lying on his cot. Rigor mortis is only supposed to last for 2-3 days but the cold temperature seemed to delay things. We were both glad that the old man's stove had gone out and the nippy February air was our friend as we flipped him onto the gurney. When we got him back to Oscar's embalming room my uncle told me, "Let's let him thaw a bit. It won't help the smell, but old man Daschel is going to be no help at all 'til those muscles relax."

I seldom did more than hand Oscar the embalming tools and occasionally helped dress a body for the visitation. One man could do the embalming but putting pants on a corpse requires some help. Some would call this a morbid way to make a living, but I believe Oscar may have been the happiest man I ever knew. People came to him when their need was greatest and Oscar had a way about him that could soothe the most broken of hearts. His humor was legendary.

He loved to travel and each night of his journeys he'd fire off a dozen post cards from places most of us had never been. I remember getting his postcard from Seattle. It said, "If it took the Lord six days and six night to make heaven and earth, I don't know why in the hell he didn't take off Thursday afternoon and leave out Utah."

We were knee deep one night in embalming Elsie Skinner when her stomach rumbled. I think it was her stomach that rumbled. It wasn't mine and Uncle Oscar swore it wasn't his. I jumped. Oscar turned to the body and said, “Elsie, you’re like my in-laws. For once I wish you’d eat before you come.”

Although we got the call soon after Frank Miller died, rigor mortis came on in a hurry, and as soon as we lifted him onto the embalming table, his left hand drew up into a fist. I nearly wet myself. Oscar looked at poor Frank’s dead face and said, “Miller, we can do this the easy way or the hard way. Now, are you gonna lie still or I do have to call your wife?”

I think the wildest Uncle Oscar tale concerned Billy Henshaw and his son Richard. They were coming home past midnight after a wild evening at the Riverview Lounge in Valley Draw and Billy lost it on Crabtree Corner. The old Pontiac took two flips to the west and smashed up against the anhydrous tanks that Sam Crabtree had parked up side of his office. Both were dead by the time Oscar arrived on the scene and he scraped up what he could find of them and loaded them into the hearse.

The Henshaws were hard-working farmers who never had any need for formal clothing, so Oscar looked into his cabinet. It wasn’t unusual in the 1940’s for a man to die without owning a suit, so Oscar would buy up whatever Henri Straus couldn’t sell at the end of the season. In one infamous incident, Henri tried to buy back one of the suits just after a visitation, saying he had a man come in and wondered where it went. Henri hated like fire to miss a sale but Oscar allowed as how once a suit was on a corpse it should probably stay.

The dead Henshaw boy was a redhead and so Oscar found a brown suit to fit the boy’s frame. He put a charcoal number on Billy who was about the same size as his son, and when the Henshaw family came that night for the pre-visitation viewing, both men looked good enough to bury. Mrs. Henshaw was a Hoerlein before she married Billy, and the Hoerleins, while good folks, were not known for their even temperaments. By the time Lola Henshaw reached the funeral home she was a slobbering wreck. Uncle Oscar quickly called for his wife Margaret to fetch some tea and crumb cake, and after thirty minutes or so Lola could breathe well enough to discuss the details of the funeral. She signed the necessary papers and her daughter was leading her out the door when the new widow suddenly turned and said, “Could I see them again?”

“Of course,” said Uncle Oscar, and he lead the two ladies back into the viewing room.

“They look very nice, Oscar. You’ve done masterful work, considering … well, you know.”

“Thank you, Lola. I’m glad you’re pleased.”

“But one thing …?”

“Lola?”

“The suits. Could you … I mean, would it be too much trouble if you changed suits?”

Oscar didn’t even blink. “Of course not, Lola. That’s no problem. When you get here tomorrow …”

“Well, I mean now. I’d really like to see them before I go home.”

“This will take a bit, Lola.”

“I’ll wait. Is there any more crumb cake, Margaret?”

Changing clothing on a dead body is one of the tougher jobs God ever gave mankind. It’s quiet, it’s peaceful, and you’re in out of the weather, but these people are no help at all. Maybe you can imagine stuffing a couple hundred pounds of jelly into a lady’s stocking. Not a single part of a corpse will cooperate and no matter where you tug, you can’t get any traction. Try putting on your shirt while lying on your back and you’ll get the idea of what this process is like if you don’t have any help. Add to this the fact that this was in Oscar’s post-leg days. If I’d been home he would have called me, but I wasn’t, and it would have been awkward to shout, “Margaret, come here and help me lift Billy’s ass high enough to slip these pants on!” with the grieving widow and daughter sitting in the next room.

So Oscar struggled.

He said it was 45 minutes and two crumb cakes later when he hobbled out of the embalming room, pushing the two caskets.

Lola looked at the bodies of her husband and her son and again burst into a Hoerlein fit of tears and wailing. Oscar had already missed Gunsmoke and his legendary good humor was nothing but an act from this point on. Lola made a rush at Oscar and collapsed, sobbing, into his arms.

This is a tricky move to make on a one-legged man. If Oscar hadn't quickly braced himself against a doorjamb, the widow, the undertaker, a half-eaten crumb cake, and the corpse would have ended up in Billy's casket. "That's okay, Lola," intoned Oscar. "It's been a rough day for everybody." Lola slowly pulled back from Oscar and looked again at her husband and her son.

"I'm upset, Oscar."

"I know you're upset, Lola. Anybody would be. It's a hard thing to go through."

"I mean … I'm so upset that I'm not talking straight … I'm not thinking clearly. You were right about the suits the first time. Can you forgive me? I'd like them changed back."

Oscar thought to himself that if he'd just omitted the pants on these two corpses he could have cut an hour off this very long evening. "It's your call, Lola. Believe me, this is no problem at all. Happens all the time." Oscar was the best. Say what you will, he kept a face to the world that anybody would have envied. "I'll have them ready for viewing tomorrow."

"Thank you, Oscar. I'm so very sorry."

"No, I'm sorry, Lola. I'm very sorry for your loss."

Lola once again got as far as the doorway when she turned and said, "I'll never be able to sleep until I see this through. Could you go ahead and change the suits now while I wait? Really. I don't mind waiting."

"But Lola …"

"Really, Oscar, it's no bother. I'm not ready to go into that empty house yet anyway."

"If you're sure it's no bother, Lola …"

"No. None at all. Perhaps I will use the restroom if you have one."

"Yes, Lola," said Oscar, "and we've even starting peeing indoors. It's that door right there."

Lola smiled at this and Uncle Oscar began wondering who he could call tomorrow morning to check out what happened to Matt Dillon. He hopped on his one leg toward the embalming room, pushing the caskets ahead of him. This old locomotive was running out of steam.

When Lola came out of the bathroom just minutes later, she opened the door to see Oscar standing there leaning on the caskets of her family members, suits changed and smiling.

"Oscar!" she exclaimed. "How … I mean, how did you switch suits so quickly?"

"Switch suits, hell. I just switched heads!"

I'm not sure that every story Uncle Oscar told was a true one, but they sure were good.

When Oscar died, he had his good friend and competitor, Bub Skinner, do the honors. Bub ran the funeral home in neighboring Valley Run and the two men were a great deal alike. Both were stalwarts in their community, both knew the value of a good laugh, and both knew how to make grieving a bit more tolerable.

At his request, Bub put a small tin plaque between Oscar's body and his long-since-departed right leg. It simply said, "Told you I was coming."

At my high school graduation party, Oscar told me, "I think you may turn out smart, but it's early to tell."

"Why's that, Uncle Oscar?"

"You know when to laugh. That's the mark of a man … what he laughs at and how hard. I think you may turn out okay." And then he laughed.

Connections

If he'd gotten up earlier that morning, Elisha Gray would have been famous. He applied for the telephone patent on the same day as Alexander Graham Bell, but Bell beat him to the patent office by a matter of hours. Bell still wasn't quite sure what he had so he hid away in a corner booth at the Centennial Exhibition in 1876, getting little attention until the Emperor Dom Pedro de Alcantara of Brazil stopped by for a chat, became amazed at the new invention, and started drawing a crowd. Emperors will do that.

It took another fifty years for the telephone to make it to Homerville, and Alice Holeman was there to welcome it. Alice was the oldest daughter of Fritz and Freida Holeman, members of the first great German immigration to the Midwest. The Holemans believed in the education of young women back before most Midwest farmers even saw a particular need for girls, beyond serving as cooks and child bearers for young men.

They shipped Alice off for two years of university at Macomb and when she returned, they rented her a small office just west of Reel's General Store, and then waited for the telephone to come to Homerville. The space wasn't more than fifteen feet wide, but it stretched all the way back to the alley some seventy-five feet. Alice had a lifelong fear of storms and high winds so she put her switchboard at the rear of the building, as far away from the plate glass windows as possible.

Or maybe it was her fear of faces. Aside from her two years at the university, Alice hadn't spent much time around people. The Holemans believed that you only left the house for church or if the house was on fire. Even then it was best to put it out and get back indoors lest the neighbors think you were being showy. In church she sat between Fritz and Freida, and it was at church where friendly conversation was frowned upon anyway. She slept in a bed next to her parents until the day she left to get an education and even her days of schooling were sheltered. Fritz found her a room above the bar at the Lamoine Hotel for what he thought was an amazingly reasonable rate. Alice later found the reason for the room's cheap rent … the bar hired a blind organist who'd play until 2 o'clock every morning and the noise would drift up through the hotel's many cracks and outright gaps. The bar would usually empty by midnight but no one ever told the organ player, and so he kept up "On the Banks of the Wabash, Far Away," "You Tell Me Your Dream," and "She Is More to Be Pitied Than Censured," until the bartender, Ervin Miller, would tap the blind musician on the shoulder and tell him that would be enough. Ervin pulled this trick because he wanted some music while cleaning up.

The fact that Alice learned to sleep with a crazed Wurlitzer only added to her sense of aloneness.

She only spoke in classes when called upon, and since her courses were mostly lecture, there was little chance of her having to say anything to anyone. After two years of learning a bit about English Literature and speaking to practically no one, Alice returned to Homerville to the news that the telephone had come to town.

Some might have thought it odd for the town's most silent woman to become the telephone operator, but Alice took to the job quickly and with some pleasure. It was always difficult to tell when Alice was enjoying herself, but those who knew her best said that her new telephone office brought a great deal of excitement to the young girl's life. The fact was, Alice did enjoy talking to people … she just had trouble looking at them. It was hard to believe that the lady on the telephone line who'd chat about the depth of the snow out your direction, the progress of your daughter's croup, and the length of the hemlines this summer in Chicago, would be the same gal who'd duck her head and look the other way if you met her on the street. If, as her Chaucer professor said was true, "The eyes are the window to the soul," then Alice would settle for a soulless existence.

The "stringers," as they were called, brought the line in from Adams and Cooperstown, then tied it right in to the Homerville office. In one long summer they had wired nearly the entire community and anybody who was or pretended to be anybody had a telephone on his kitchen wall. Alice started out with a ten switch board in June and by August she manned a board with over forty plugs and wires. And of course everyone was on a party line, ranging from a six-jack line to a twelve. Each subscriber had a coded ring … two longs and one short … three shorts and one long … and when the phone rang, everyone picked up.

If you had an important call to make you had to talk fast since each time a new listener picked up the phone the signal would grow weaker. Our ring was a short, a long, and a final short. It became the family signal as Dad would pull up to a crowded schoolyard at the end of the day and give a short-long-short blast on his horn. We knew the signal so Kelly and I would come running. When we'd go to bed at night, Dad would bang the short-long-short through the wall with his shoe. We'd holler back, "'Night Dad! Night Mom!"

Mabel Walker, who traded in egg futures, raised two and a half children, and washed paper plates before she threw them away was probably the worst about eavesdropping. She'd leave a radio program or interrupt her prayers if she heard the neighbor's ring. The very thought of anything happening in the universe without her being privy to it was more than Mabel Walker could bear. When she asked, "How are you?" she meant it and she wanted a detailed answer. My Grandmother Marie detested Mabel's habit of listening in to every conversation, so Grandma hatched a plan. She called Flo Meserve and asked for the recipe for rhubarb cherry pie. Flo began to list the ingredients, "… one cup of shortening and three-quarters cup of water …" Mabel was listening in and her sense of place and purpose couldn't take it. She knew that the recipe called for three-quarters cup of shortening and one cup of water so she spoke up and told them so. There was a long silence on the phone then Grandma and Flo heard Mabel's embarrassed click.

Alice Holeman lived with her parents until Freida died of heart failure and then Fritz finally succumbed to loneliness and jumped into a very cold Illinois River one night just before the ice locked it tight. Alice saw no need to ramble around the big old family homestead alone so she sold the place and built an apartment over the telephone office. She had Johnny Johnson build a set of stairs leading directly from her bedroom to the switchboard, so unless she was going to church or the apartment caught fire, she wouldn't have to meet a soul face to face. She was not showy.

In fact, in appearance Alice resembled a slender, laced nun. Her high fringed collar, her tiny eyeglasses posed precariously on the tip of her nose, the starch in her plain black woolen skirt, and her blonde hair bunned up so tight that it looked like a golden fist balanced atop a perfectly proportioned head … all combined to make an admirable if wholly unattainable package.

Everyone knew that Alice listened to most phone conversations. This was a given and seemed only right. After all, her hand was on the plugs and it was important to get yourself unplugged if you were going to get your next call. Far from being an intrusion, this covered Homerville with a certain sense of security. We knew that as long as Alice was listening, the conversations would be kept on the up and up. You didn't cuss, you only dabbled in gossip when it was needful, and without any design or purposeful plan, Alice had become God. Sort of. God heard everything and Alice heard everything. God was moral and Alice seemed every bit as upright as the Almighty. Nothing was hidden from the eyes of God and little escaped the ears of Alice. And like God, she didn't exactly ask for the job … shortly after the creation of the party line it was thrust upon her. In the beginning was Alice and that was just fine with us. God was just and so, we supposed, was Alice. It made you feel safe to retire of an evening knowing that Alice's ear was still poised at the receiver.

Of course, Alice would sometimes travel the fourteen steps from her front door to the Reel Brothers Grocery and it was very much like God walking. You'd step around Hank Reel's meat counter and see Alice there waiting for a pound of ground chuck and … well, you knew that she knew everything about you … not only what you knew about you but what everyone else knew as well. And like God, it was both comforting and terrifying to come face to face with her.

And it was this very holiness and awe that compounded the confusion when Alice, single and sanctified, came up pregnant.

The chatter factory was stoked into full-throttle as the news spread around Homerville. You could look at a couple of folks stopped across the street and read Alice's story being reenacted in their gestures.

J.D. Lahr's Meat Market:

"She can't be. That's impossible."

"They say it's true."

"Then I suppose it is."

"But how … She never even speaks to people face to face."

"You tell me. I mean, that's one thing you can't really do over the telephone."

Rob and Ferd's Barbershop:

"You do it, Ferd?"

"Don't think I ain't thought about it. You seen the way she shakes that little package?"

"My old woman says it must of been immaculate reception."

"Looks like she made one connection too many."

The Methodist Guild:

"You just never know, do you?"

"We all fall. Some harder than others."

"We don't all fall like that."

"Judge not, lest ye …"

"Why not?"

"I suppose you're right."

And while the town rumbled with puzzlement, Alice took her daily station at the switchboard, only answering with her usual polite "Thank You," when someone asked for long distance.

Meanwhile, her lovers kept changing faces and motivations.

Tuesday morning had it that he was a stranger … someone from Quincy or Valley or Martinsburg. By Tuesday afternoon he'd become a salesman who, rumor had it, was in line to inherit a great deal of money. His fortune, combined with the money Fritz and Freida left behind, would probably be enough to move to Minnesota where people can get lost. By Wednesday noon the child's father was Carl Reel who had been seen delivering Alice's groceries one afternoon when she … so she said … didn't have time to leave the office. Carl did everything quickly and with a smile, and he was always quick to oblige anyone in need.

Thursday's father was Berg Clifford, the mayor. Berg deemed it his official duty to check in with each of Homerville's businesses at least once a week and some said he even had a key to the telephone office. It rained hard Friday and left the town with only the telephone for communication so the child was fatherless until the sun came out about 8 o'clock Saturday morning when it was discovered that Alice had probably been held against her will by Lap Toosman, the town drunk. Lap would often wonder aimlessly and more than once ended up in the wrong house at bedtime, but we never knew him to have his way with anyone but his niece and, as they said, "Hell, she was half dippy anyway."

And the funny thing … or least it seemed funny to us … is that Alice made no attempt to hide her delicate condition. Traffic would slow to a curious crawl when she'd make her twice-a-week strolls to the grocery store, her skirt stretched tight over her expanding motherhood. "You'd think," it was said, "she'd have the decency to hide it a bit." But she didn't.

When Doc Denney answered her call around five one evening, the main drag looked like a parade. People were parked nearly the entire western length of the business district, and when he came out the door, buttoning his coat, every head turned.

Births in Homerville are semi-public events. The details of length, weight, sex, hair color, and disposition of the mother are immediately broadcast like the weather report. Doc lumbered down the first of the two concrete steps leading to the street and before he stepped in his car he turned and shouted, "It's a boy!"

Horns honked, children cheered, a hat or two flew into the air, and Lap Toosman woke up from a two-day drunk. It was like Christmas with warm weather. Alma Henthorn ran up and grabbed the doctor's car door. "Does she need help?" she asked.

Doc shook his head. "Oh, I think she'll be fine. Her husband's seein' to her nicely. Thank you, though." Alma's face crumbled with disappointment, which is exactly what Doc expected and wanted.

Her husband? A quick head count was made of every man on the street. Some seemed disappointed, and a few worried wives breathed a sigh of relief. Hank Reel excused himself and took a wide path through the town park to see what automobile might be parked behind the telephone office. Carl Reel turned to his wife, smiled and began repeating, "Told ja, told ja, told ja."

There's a limit to how long you can stare at a darkened building, even in Homerville. What used to be the town's most nondescript building was now the House of Mystery. After twenty minutes or so the street began to empty of its gawkers and most drifted off to digest, speculate, and wonder. It was a temptation, of course, to start calling the neighbors since Alice was surely taking the day off from her switchboard. Raymond Mitchell, a retired widower, was Alice's assistant and he would most certainly be the operator for a few days. Raymond was purely and hilariously awful at the job. If you asked for a connection, your chances for success were about one in three. Oh, you'd be connected but to Lord knew whom. Raymond's eyesight had prevented him from getting a driver's license for the past two years and now he had the frustrating job of reading Alice's dainty handwritten labels above each plug receptacle. This was not a major problem in Homerville unless it was an emergency. When Raymond would connect you with the wrong party you like as not knew them and there was good probability that you'd be related. In any case, you always had a good chat.

Alice's mystery deepened the next afternoon when the Wells Fargo truck stopped in front of the telephone office with three boxes marked "Becker-Ryan & Co., Halsted and 63rd, Chicago, Illinois," then scrawled in charcoal marking pencil, "Baby clothes."

Doc Denney was the last of the old-time country doctors. He'd pull a calf or doctor your pigs for mastitis on Monday morning, then deliver a baby that evening. Doc was midwife, surgeon, market analyst, vet, priest and marriage counselor. He worked mostly in trade during the Depression and in fact, he made a much better living off eggs, timber, and sides of beef than he did when cash became available again in the forties. He bought his present home with a load of hedge posts when a very drunk Morey Lanner overpaid him one night for two day's hog castration. When Doc Denney died he was owed money by nearly everyone in Homerville. As soon as Mrs. Denney got home from burying him, she took all his old due notices out in the alley and burned them.

She said that Doc had provided well for her and that it was his wish that all bills be marked paid when he passed on.

If Alice was God … a position that began to slip at the birth of her out-of-wedlock baby, then Doc Denney was Saint Peter. His know-all position had given him a certain status in Homerville, and he wisely kept his mouth shut about nearly everything he saw and heard. The good citizens of the town knew it was useless to ask him the details of the new baby he'd just delivered, but that didn't keep a few from trying. Everybody bought Doc coffee that week. Berg Clifford picked up the tab for his lunch. And every conversation began the same way …

"So Doc … hear you had a birthin' this week."

"Yep."

"Everybody okay?"

"Like cake."

"And the dad … I suppose he's …"

"I suppose he is."

And that was as far as you got with Doc Denney. No mention of who the father was, how he'd come to know Alice, and where in the heck the fellow was. It had now been four days and no one had entered or left the building except the Wells Fargo man and Raymond Mitchell, and there was no use quizzing Raymond. Aside from being only half bright and unable to hear loud thunder, Raymond lived in a hazy world of oatmeal cookies and Zane Gray novels. If the world ended on Saturday, it would be the middle of the next week before Raymond heard about it.

"He's got to come out sometime," Isabelle Wilson told her husband Leonard. "That's only a one room apartment and there's three of them countin' the baby."

"How do you know they're still there?" asked Leonard.

"Whatta you mean?"

"They could have slipped out in the middle of the night." This was a flummoxing thought to Isabelle. She hadn't considered that. The only thing that she and the rest of Homerville hated worse than a mystery was an unsolved mystery.

The mystery might have gone unsolved for years if Fritz Holeman hadn't showed up late that fall. We were all, of course, surprised to see him. Not only did we assume that he was dead … most of us had even attended the memorial service … but even when he was living in Homerville he just didn't get out that much.

And of course no one was more surprised to see her dead father walking through the front door than Alice Holeman.

Fritz Holeman was a man of few words but this seemed to be a time when at least some explanation was needed. Alice had little luck.

"Papa! Oh my God! Papa! Are you really Papa?"

"Where's the child?" Fritz was soft-spoken.

"But my God, Papa! You aren't dead?"

"Is he sleepin'? I don't want to wake him."

Alice grabbed at her chest. "I've got to sit down."

"Fine. You look a little pale, Alice. Is the baby upstairs?"

"He's … yes … he's right up the stairs. But …"

But Fritz was up the stairs in three strides, his long, German legs taking the steps in slow, easy strides.

Alice could hear him talking to his "little man" and his "fine big boy" through the open door.

The average citizen of lower Illinois will not stop and gawk at a car wreck. If you tell him your right arm is slowly being infected by a tropical disease he won't inquire any further information unless you care to elaborate. He is curious, of course, but the thought of seeming meddlesome is just below incest and voting Democrat on his list of sins. However, on the day Fritz Holeman came back to life, drove to Homerville and parked his Chevy roadster right in front of the telephone office, then walked right in, the heretofore reserved citizenry of Homerville became Chicagoans. Every available nose in Homerville was plastered against the big glass windows of the phone company.

Alice's day had already gotten off to an unusual start when her dead father walked into the phone office and inquired about her baby. When she swiveled her operator's chair around and saw half the nostrils in Homerville sucking the polish off her windows, it was more than she could stand. She stood, she gently straightened her skirt, then she picked up the latest (and heaviest) volume of "The Official List of Telephone Exchanges for the United States and Canada." and hurled it against the west window.

I have always marveled at the natural herding instinct in people. Even folks who don't know each other will exhibit a sort of communal magnet. The elderly will cluster with the elderly, the teens with the teens, farmers with farmers, and attractive people with those of similar comeliness. In Homerville we react on a denominational basis and as the fates would have it, the Methodists had congregated up against the east window while the Presbyterians assembled on the west. As the day's events were counted and recounted in years to come, the Methodists always swore it was the hand of God that intervened and sent the 8-pound phone directory hurtling toward the Presbyterians, and the Presbyterians swore it was divine interference that kept the window from breaking and cutting John Calvin's descendents to predestined smithereens.

In short, the book bounced off the window and onto the floor. Alice, after a moment's reasoning, thought this to be just as well. It scattered the crowd but it saved the window. She'd had enough problems for one day.

By the time Fritz came down the stairs, holding the sleeping Fritz, Jr. in his arms, the throng had retreated to the middle of the street. There was some talk of calling the police but after Berg Clifford took only a few hurried steps toward the café's phone, he stopped and allowed as how coming back from the dead wasn't a crime … at least as far as he could remember.

"He's a fine boy, Alice." Fritz smiled and sat down on the steps, gently rolling the baby's tiny toes between his calloused fingers.

"He's quite remarkable, Papa."

"I'm very happy for you, little girl."

"Papa … this is all so … I mean, you must …"

"I heard about the baby. All the way from Alton. Ain't that somethin'? All the way from Alton. The Wells-Fargo man was tellin' the story and I knew it had to be you."

"But …"

"Couldn't drown, Alice. Tried, but … hell … kept poppin' up … even in the cold water. You ever try to … no, I suppose you haven't. Hell, it's hard to drown. Just keep poppin' up."

"But why didn't you …?"

"Not smart. No good reason, Alice. I just wasn't smart. When I came ashore I was still in sight of the Meredosia bridge, but by that time … I don't know. I just had to get away. And then you stay away awhile longer and then some longer still … and before long you've stayed away so long it'd be shameful to come back. But that wasn't smart."

"I … I don't know what to say, Papa. I love you. Mama loved you. And little Fritz …"

"Fritz?"

"I named him after you, Papa. But I had no idea you two would ever meet up this side of heaven."

"Well, Homerville's for sure this side of heaven … and …" tears were filling the old man's eyes, "… and we have now met up." Fritz had never cried in front of Alice. He'd never cried in front of any woman. Now he looked at his beautiful daughter and he wept openly … a good, smiling cry. "And my dear God but am I happy, Alice! My dear God am I glad I came back!" His body was shaking with the weeping and baby Fritz let out a disturbed yell that startled the old man. "And my dear God but ain't that just about the best sound I ever heard!"

Alice told him about Mrs. Meserve and how her son from Peoria would call every night to check on his mother's frail condition … of how Alice would call the elderly lady in the afternoons to gauge the old lady's condition so her son would know what to say that evening. She told Fritz how when Mrs. Meserve died, Paul had stopped to thank her for the kindnesses shown his mother, how they agreed to see each other on his trips across the state to take care of the estate, how one thing lead to another …

Fritz understood, and he was mightily grateful that Paul had left provision for Alice's care when he returned to his wife and children in Peoria. "When Doc Denney left that evening he told everybody that the father was taking care of things. The whole town thinks I've had some man holed up here for weeks and they're dying to see who walks out the front door."

"It must be difficult, Alice. I mean, in a small town and all."

"It is. But others have their burdens as well. Paul and I are sorry. We've asked God for forgiveness, and in spite of that we'll probably carry the guilt with us to our graves, but little Fritz … he shares none of that, Papa."

"No. I guess not. And it's no worse than jumping in a river."

The mother, the grandpa, spent a long moment just looking at the baby who'd now awakened completely and had discovered a new and wonderful fascination with the buttons on Fritz Sr.'s denim coat.

On March 10 of 1891, Almon Strowger, an undertaker in Topeka, Kansas, patented the strowger switch, a device that eventually lead to the dialing telephone. Almon was somewhat of a paranoid who thought that operators were sending his calls to his competitors. Fifty years later the device made its way to Homerville and the party lines began to give way to the dial telephone. Then, from the dial telephone the progress was swift to the private line.

Lap Toosman

There are mean drunks and then there are the others. Lap Toosman was one of the others. Were the facts known, I suppose that Lap didn't drink as much as several other residents of Homerville but the man had the audacity to be drunk in public instead of behind closed doors like the rest of the drinkers. He was a public drunk and the town had trouble abiding public drunks. Like a strange uncle you only see once at Christmas, you acknowledge his presence but wish to God he belonged to somebody else.

Lap was a day laborer in the days when working by the job, by the day, was common. Every town had its share of men who'd be willing to work a day for a day's pay then shuffle off to some other job tomorrow. They didn't make much money but living in Central Illinois in the thirties didn't require any large income. In fact, although day work may have been far from noble, it was respected and needed. When a man put up hay or had hogs to castrate or corn to plow, he needed a man or two even though he couldn't afford to hire them full time. So that was Lap's fate and his life's work, toiling day by day for somebody or other and unless the roads were just too impassable to get to town, there was always somebody willing to hire him. We had a few others … Roley Dinsmore, Pop Wilson, Abe Tunley … but they came and went. Lap was as much a fixture as the bandstand.

Of course the bandstand was more solid and you could depend on it being there the next morning. With Lap you really never knew. If he needed the money badly and you gave him at least a day's notice, he'd likely show up on the front stoop of the hotel, ready to work. If he had enough cash to buy a case of Falstaff or you caught him in the morning and expected him to buck bales that afternoon, you might as well look for somebody else.

Lap was a tall, gangly fellow who could have done a passable impersonation of Lincoln given a couple more inches, a few more pounds, and a bit more brain. He lived on the ground floor of the Homerville Hotel, but by the time he stumbled in at night, he'd completely forgotten which room was his. Ma Runkel never locked any of the rooms and the beds were similar in their lumpy terrain, so wherever Lap lit, Lap lit.

Lap didn't drive so he'd depend on whoever was hiring him to get him to the job, and he'd depend even more desperately for Luke at the implement company to bring him his booze from Valley every few days. Sometimes Luke had to bring him the stuff on credit, but he generally required cash. He liked old Lap and he knew that if he didn't keep working the man could become a problem to all of us.

Berg Clifford, our mayor, had it about right when he said, "You know, boys …" (Berg always started everything with "You know, boys …" He was elected mayor of Homerville the same day that Richard Daley became mayor of Chicago and both men immediately adopted a patronizing tone that let everyone know he was mayor.) "You know, boys," Berg would say, "every town needs a drunk. It gives a village a sense of balance. For every saint there's got to be a sinner and Lap provides us with the necessary equilibrium." Nothing that Berg Clifford said ever made much sense but he had a way of saying it that made you feel you were standing at the feet of Moses at Mt. Sinai. We appreciated him for that. It was impressive in a time when inspiration was sometimes all we had.

Although the town drunk can often be the butt of many jokes … and Lap was that as well … the older members of the community had a real soft spot in their heart for the old boozer. They remembered when the Toosmans came to town and started the village's first restaurant, a sort of adjunct to the hotel and a place that turned a real profit before the Depression. Lee Toosman was a businessman with a keen ear to what folks wanted and his wife Maria was a good cook who could turn out the beans in quantity without sacrificing a smidgeon of taste. She always said, "It's all in the spicing and you either know spicing or you don't." They had two boys. Waldo went on to college, stayed single, and taught physics at the University of Missouri. Then there was Henry who got the name "Lap" from his days as a track star for Homerville High.

And he was good. More than good some said. Those long, sinewy legs of his were the terror of track and he set as many records in dashes as he did in the distance events. You'll still find his name on an imitation gold plaque outside the boys' locker room. The kids see it today and laugh, not being able to imagine how a man who stumbles over sidewalk cracks and was forever landing on his face in front of the hotel could have once left other runners in his dust. So it goes. Where Lap lit, he lit.

When Lee Toosman died he left the café business to Maria but she soon moved to Columbia to live with Waldo and told Lap he could have the business if he wanted it. He thought a minute then told her that, no, he didn't believe he was cut out for cooking and clearing tables, so she sold the restaurant to Norma Dix and left Lap enough of a bank account to pay his rent for as long as he wanted to stay in Homerville.

And now comes the gap. Nothing is known of Christ's life between the ages of 3 and 30, so there is a precedent for a man's development becoming a mystery. Many concerned folks pondered long and hard on what would make a strapping young man with good folks and somewhat of a future become the town's most notable drunk. We knew he had promise and we knew he'd wasted it, but as to what caused the change … well, speculation is the chief occupation of small town residents so we were well employed during the last years of Lap's life.

Some men drink to forget their sorrows, but Lap had no more sorrows than the next fellow. Some drink in order to gain the courage they can't summon on their own but Lap Toosman seemed as confident and intelligent as any young man in his youth. A family history of boozing is often the culprit in an old drunk's past, but Lee and Maria were both teetotalers … conservative Calvinists who believed that if things were meant to be, they were meant to be … and Lap never knew the rest of his family. It seemed that alcoholism was an idea he'd come up with on his own. And like many drunks, Lap was generous.

There wasn't a young boy or girl on the streets of Homerville who hadn't been a recipient of a nickel or dime when Lap would stop to pat them on the head and inquire about their day. I received many myself although I always assumed by the pressure that Lap would put on my head that he was not so much patting as trying to steady himself. A ten year old is just about the right height for a leaning post.

Whenever it was time to set up the benches for the town's annual Pioneer Day celebration, Lap was the first man in line to haul boards. Whenever the volunteer fire department was called into action in the middle of the night, Lap would be the first man at the station. Of course, they kept him sitting in the fire truck since at that time of night he was in no shape to skinny up a ladder. In fact, Lap was often the one who first spotted the fire and rang the bell, being the only resident of Homerville who was awake at that time of night. Rumor was, because of his fondness for Lucky Strikes unfiltered he was actually the cause of many of the fires so it was only right that he should report them and help put them out.

If you had a death in the family, he'd be among the first mourners to stop by and offer his regrets, sometimes leaving an envelope with a couple of dollars. He regularly mowed the yard for every widow who needed a hand and he was pretty good at slapping paint on houses as long as it didn't require too much ladder work. This never stopped Lap from climbing ladders but he nearly always fell and with him, at least a gallon of good paint. You'd drive by a freshly painted house, see a large splotch of white grass and know that Lap had found himself some work that day.

And somebody's got to dig the graves. Never known as a particularly noble occupation, grave digging often gets relegated to whoever needs the money the worst. Lap considered it not only pleasant work … outdoors, lots of fresh air, pretty surroundings, no one alive to bother you … but a public service. The undertaker, Uncle Oscar, would hunt Lap down in one of his usual haunts and say, "Got a diggin' Lap," and Lap would nod his head and ask for the particulars. Lap had to listen closely since he couldn't read well. Learning disabilities were written off as mere "slowness" when Lap attended school and many young folks graduated by the oral method, reciting as little as was required to the kindest teacher they could find, then grabbing their diploma and hoping to God that nobody ever asked much of them. So when Oscar would give the whereabouts of a gravesite, Lap would listen with careful attention. After all, he knew the town's cemetery pretty well and when the sun was up and he was sober he could tell north from south. Oscar would say, "Just south of the big Henderson stone there's three lots and this is the middle one."

This worked middling well when Lap was sober so Oscar made every effort to contact Lap personally and take a good look at his eyes. A couple of times he had to leave notes with Ma Runkel at the hotel and between her loony mind and Lap's sometimes inebriated state, the graves were dug in the wrong spot. This means an extra afternoon's work of filling in the hole if the lot is empty. If it's occupied there are other things to consider.

Although Hank Reel would take Lap a new set of clothing every Christmas, Lap would forever wear the same pair of stained denim overalls with the left strap missing. He'd draw himself a map of the gravesite and take off west toward the cemetery with the paper in his left front pocket. If the bereaved family was lucky, he didn't stop off anywhere on the way. If Floyd Hammit invited him in for a Falstaff then the grave would get dug a bit later and sometimes in the right spot. Oscar said that on the first mistake he found, the deceased still had a perfectly preserved silk necktie around the neck of the skeleton. Everything was rotted away but the bones and the silk. Metal caskets had yet to come into general use and burial vaults were only for the extremely well-heeled corpses, so even the wooden frame would have been worm meal by the time Lap's shovel bit into the grave. It was the joke around town that whenever a graveside minister would intone something about "final resting place," the local wags would always smile and mutter, "that is, if Lap stays sober."

Winter is the gravedigger's most bitter enemy as the frozen ground seldom gives up its hold without a struggle … or in Lap's case, a stick of dynamite. Gravediggers were allowed to purchase and carry dynamite in those days and a half-stick was usually enough to start a hole and get a bite on the grave. Lap knew how to use dynamite and although it might have frightened some unknowing souls to have the town drunk walking down the street with dynamite in his overalls, the residents of Homerville saw it as the normal run of things. After all, he kept his matches in his left front pocket and his dynamite in his left rear. The match would have to burn through Lap's leg for any real damage to be done.

Viona Lacksheide had died before the days when antibiotics would have most likely saved her. It wasn't uncommon then to simply die of a bad cold and that's what she did. She and Fred had wisely picked out their lot on the north side of the cemetery right next to Dean Lahr's sawmill since it was on a nice slope and had good drainage. Viona thought drainage was important in the afterlife. Some twenty years later Fred decided to join her. At least we think it was his decision. He was healthy as a bull and drinking coffee at the café one day then dead the next morning … a January morning. Cold as a witch's heart. The ground began to freeze toward the middle of December, and the frost had crept to nearly a foot into the ground when Oscar found Lap sitting behind the Village Inn sleeping off a drunk, huddled up against the exhaust fan from the kitchen. He woke Lap, told him to get inside before he froze to death, and then explained the whereabouts of Fred Lachsheide's grave. "Do you hear me good, Lap?"

"Got 'er, Oscar."

"You sober? I'll come see you tomorrow morning if you're feelin' puny this afternoon."

"Nope. I can see the grave in my mind. Right west of the sawmill."

"That's it!" Oscar was pleased and satisfied that Lap knew where to dig. "But don't mess with Viona."

"Nope. Dug her grave 20 years ago, April the fourteenth and it rained all day. You buried her with her red hat on."

How could you doubt this accurate a description? Oscar helped Lap to his feet and took him in the back door where Marietta LaTeur was just finishing her last piano lesson of the day. "See that he stays sober, Marietta," Oscar told her.

She grinned. "Yes, I'll take him home with me and stick him in the cupboard overnight."

Of course all these precautions went for nothing when Lap lit the fuse the next morning and blew Viona Lackscheide all over the sawmill.

Viona did in fact inhabit the first metal vault that Oscar ever sold in Homerville. It was probably the best-attended graveside service the town had ever seen as many folks showed up just to see the shiny grey burial chamber lowered into the ground. Oscar said that the Charleston-Trigard Vault Company printed in its literature that the thing was waterproof, vermin-proof, and heat resistant, but that it didn't mention anything about dynamite. Whether Lap was drunk that morning or not was immaterial. The fact was that Oscar had a mess on his hands and as he rushed his Oldsmobile down to the cemetery he had a short, terse conversation with God about the timing of letting the town's first metal vault coincide with Lap's dynamite. When Oscar pulled up Cemetery Hill he saw the form of Lap's overalls bending and picking something up along the fence that separated the sawmill and the graveyard. In fact, Lap had gathered a bushel basketful of items as he continued to pick things out of the fencerow.

Oscar walked over to Lap and said, "Well, damn it, Lap. You've blown Viona all over hell, haven't you?"

"'Spect I have," said Lap. "Dern sorry. This is her, isn't it?" He held a piece of crimson felt out for Oscar's inspection.

"Yep. The hat. What else you got in your basket?"

Oscar and Lap spent the rest of the morning sorting out pieces of Viona. By noon most of the town had heard of the lady's premature resurrection and had wandered down to the cemetery to help pick through the grass for what they could salvage of her. A few years before Oscar died he told someone that his sale of vaults exploded after that day. From what they could find of Viona the town decided that the things did indeed preserve the body somewhat … at least for twenty years.

Oscar wrapped what could be found of Viona in a rubber refuse container from his embalming supplies and tucked it discretely under Fred's arm in the casket. Reverend Hammond did what amounted to a double service at the gravesite and even Lap stood in the back row of mourners to show his respects. Lap could drink away practically anything, including any sense of remorse or guilt. He was raised a strict Calvinist and assumed that some things were just meant to be.

Pastor Ann

Pastor Ann opened the box and smiled a sigh. The shimmering rainbow-hued vestment had mysteriously appeared on the floor outside the church office on the second week of her appointment. Paisley ... she thought. I haven't seen paisley since college.

This Easter … this will be the Easter I wear it. It will fit my message most wonderfully. And besides, she thought, how could anything possibly cause more trouble?

Pastor Ann was the Homerville Methodists' first female minister. In fact, she was the first lady preacher ever in Homerville. On the political spectrum, the Presbyterians were known as being the most left leaning, and the Disciples of Christ had a firm hold on the right wing. The Methodists were somewhere in the middle and fluttered back and forth between the two opposing wings, depending upon the temperament of the current pastor and the current inhabitant of the White House.

Pastor Ann suffered the twin handicaps of being both female and intelligent. Either burden would have been enough to make her tenure uncomfortable but the double whammy was a constant weight upon her ministry. Being attractive only added to her troubles.

She'd promised herself … she'd promised God … that this Easter would be her coming-out sermon. For once she'd stand up there with no fear of censure and give exactly the message that God had laid upon her heart. The sermon needed little preparation. She'd been working on it for fifteen years.

It was entitled "I'll take my Jesus dancing!" … the best sermon she'd never given. It began with a poem she'd written one night beside a bass pond:

My Jesus sings, My Jesus smiles, My Jesus taps his feet with joy.
Daring birds to match his tenor ... Taunting meadowlarks to join ...
Bringing crows into the contest ...
His head tossed back in gales of laughter, His eyes convulsed to joyous squints ...
And when he laughs, the mountains answer, When he roars, the hills respond ...
And when he dances ... Jesus dances ... all creation joins the chorus.
I'll take my Jesus dancing, mountain high and treetop tall ...
Dancing with the wind beneath him, Dancing with the sun around him,
Moonlight dancing, sparrow dancing, barefoot tickling water dancing,
Dancing through the prairie summer, Dancing o'er the lakes of winter
Jumping, Floating, whirlwind making,
I'll take him ... take my Jesus dancing.

Get down, J-man! Let them see you! Tapping out the tune of Glory!
Sidestep all the piety so lightly ...
Do it, J-man! Do it lightly ... stop the show ... bring down the house!
Awed, BoJangles smiles in envy ... Cowed, Astaire shouts "Do it, Baby!"

Clog with all the love that's in ya, Rock-a-bye my baby blue note! Tip the lights and rock creation ... Dance it, J-man! Let them feel it!

And laughing ... did you hear that? Laughing?
Laughing like the lark was holy! Laughing, gut-bust, ribble-tickling,
Laughing from a new-found depth of joy now
Laughing ... deep and gutsy roaring ...
Laughing as all fear is beaten!
Laughing! Laughing! Laughing! ...... Dancing!

Pastor Ann put down her pen. It had happened again. How many times had she been in mid-composition when she saw Wanda's face? Wanda sat in the next-to-last pew, left side, exactly 18 inches from the armrest. If some hapless stranger stumbled into church before she got there and had sat himself in the next-to-last pew, left side, exactly 18 inches from the armrest, Wanda would first stare, then clear her throat, and if all else failed, ask him to move.

Mark Twain had a name for her ... the Moral Popper. Wanda was the watchdog for the town's morality.

Wanda knew every thou-shalt-not in the King James Version and felt like the newer translations were Satan's attempt to water down the gospel. The older wags in town knew that Wanda was just about the hottest little number to walk down the street in the '50's and in order to completely cleanse herself of sin and repent of her wayward youth, the whole town would have to submit to her Methodist style of purgatory.

And despite this, Wanda was an uncommonly nice lady. She dispensed venom with a smile of Christian understanding and genuine pity. When she pointed out that your daughter's bare midriff would likely lead to a life of drugs and prostitution, you almost wanted to thank her. When Wanda mentioned that you had missed Sunday School during the entire month of July and that she had the records to prove it, her grin nearly made you want to thank her for pointing it out.

Wanda was a scorekeeper. Most folks were of the notion that if she'd somehow have the chance to have Christ over for coffee (decaf only) that she'd warm him up a bit with pleasant conversation then ask him if his theory of forgiveness for just anyone wasn't a bit … well … too liberal. What good after all was it to keep score of people's transgressions if Jesus was going to just come along and forgive everything? What would be Wanda's purpose in life?

Every time Pastor Ann began to compose a sermon on the sheer joy of following Christ, Wanda's face came to mind. For Wanda, the Christian walk was an obligation … a duty … and one that only she and perhaps a few others could manage to tread without stumbling. What good was heaven if they'd let just anybody in?

Pastor Ann was raised on a small farm in Texas, grew up wrestling her older brothers for the right to take a bath while the water was still warm, and through an odd series of events ended up as an accountant in Nashville, Tennessee, at the age of 22. She wanted to become a teacher, she'd toyed with being a writer, she appeared in several plays in college, and one of her professors told her that she had a future in music. So Ann became an accountant. She was daddy's girl and daddy said, "Enjoy your pastimes, but get a degree that pays."

Ann hated accounting and she was the best accountant in Anderson and Anderson's stable of number jugglers. She was more than smart, she was good with people, and she loved to travel. Then one morning Ann woke up in the Comfort Inn of West Nashville with a killer hangover and decided to enter the ministry. When she was four years old her grandmother had dragged her to a tent rival in a pasture outside Tyler, and in spite of her various career musings, Ann always had a feeling this would happen. "You can fight when the Lord calls," she remembers her Grandmother saying, "but he will never quit wrestlin' until you give in … or die."

Grandma Doris was Ann's hero. Doris Morgan was a tart-tongued cow wrestler and steer puncher for fifty-five years until she formally became a Christian. Her heart had changed but her steer-stained language had become so much a part of her that it hung on. Ann could still remember Doris's Christmas prayer, "Lord, it's been a hell of a year and I'll be damned if I can see any good that's come of it, but by God, we're here and we thank you for what we're about to eat. Amen!"

It took all the composure Ann's family could muster to keep straight faces when Grandma Doris prayed. But in many ways, Doris was the most genuine Christian Ann had ever met. Unlike the souls that were to people Ann's life in the ministry, Grandma Doris laid her cards on the table. She firmly believed that church was for sinners and saints not only need not apply, but frankly, they were tedious if not downright boring.

Unlike the carefully carved and mounted prayers Ann heard from the small-town Texas pulpits, Grandma Doris's prayers were worth listening to … for both their honestly and their color. One night as she tucked Ann into bed, Doris sat on the edge of her granddaughter's covers and said, "Let's pray, little girl." Ann closed her eyes and waited … nothing happened. She finally whispered, "Grandma, aren't you going to pray?" Doris kept her eyes shut and said, "No. Tonight I'm just listening. He already knows what's on my mind. I wanna find out what he's thinking."

In fact, most of Grandma's praying was done standing up, feet on the ground and eyes wide open. She'd look right at Ann over a plate of bacon and eggs and say, "Lord, this little girl's got a burden on her heart today. She won't tell me what it is, so I'm expecting you to fix it."

Grandma didn't ask God for favors. She expected him to act as he promised. This was so biblical that it shocked most people and completely embarrassed the local clergy.

Ann always had the sneaking feeling that after a day of hearing the world's begging and pleading and moaning, he was glad to hear Grandma Doris's forthright pronouncements. "How would it make you feel," said Doris once to her Sunday school class, "if your best friend felt like she had to beg and plead with you for the smallest favor? Shoot, I ain't about to insult God by groveling. We're amigos!" The leader of the class decided it was time for prayer and a quick dismissal.

When Ann entered college she asked Grandma Doris if she'd write down a simple statement of her faith … a sort of "faith diary" on her years on the Texas plains. Grandma Doris, then tucked firmly into a Tyler nursing home, snorted, "And just who in the hell would want to read that?"

Ann spent two years both confounding and delighting her seminary professors with questions like, "But if we do good to please God, doesn't that mean we want his favor? And if we want his favor, aren't be doing good for selfish reasons?"
and …
"Can we ever forgive if we cannot forget?"
and …
"If the whole point of Christianity is getting to spend eternity with Christ, then isn't Christianity an extremely self-centered religion?"

She graduated with honors, with relief, and with a great desire to simply find a small corner of the world and minister by example. "Protestant nun-ship," she once called it. Soon after seminary she gave up on the dream of a monkish existence when she met Doug the lawyer. They married in the chapel where she had been ordained and he agreed to follow her in the nomadic ways of the Methodist ministry, and after a few appointments to multi-church charges, she ended up in Homerville.

The local District Superintendent of Methodism deemed Homerville ready to enter the 20th century and have its first female ministry. It wasn't the most wrong-headed judgment he ever made but it ranked in the top five.

Midwest Methodism, like the structures in many mainline denominations, is governed by the merit system. The hierarchy of the church promises to "prayerfully consider" all appointments, then, as if by spiritual magic, the better ministers get promoted to the larger churches that can pay more. Small, rural churches are the farm teams to the big leagues, staffed by young ministers on their way up or older pastors heading toward retirement. Hypocrisy aside, it was a workable system and everyone knew the unwritten rules. If you wanted good preaching then you had to pay the price.

Pastor Ann was still new in the system when she was traded to the Homerville farm club. "You're the perfect lady to break them in," the superintendent told her. "They're a free-thinking congregation and I think you'll be a perfect match."

And Ann believed that. Why not? Women ran most rural churches, they owned over fifty percent of the county's farmland, and Ann fully expected to see a female President in her lifetime. What could possibly be the problem with having a lady minister?

She found out at her first meeting of the Pastor Relations Committee.

"The roses outside your office. That'll be your job to tend them."

"The … excuse me?"

"They were all donated by the families of deceased members in honor of their loved ones. It wouldn't look very good to have them die … the flowers, that is."

Ann had her Grandmother's forthrightness. "Did … uh … did my predecessors … the former ministers ..."

"They were all men."

And there, in a doomsday nutshell, lie Pastor Ann's fate in Homerville. All men were created equal. The ladies tended to the flowers.

Oh, she had her fans. But most were under twenty-one and didn't sit on church committees. For thirty years, the Homerville Methodist youth drooped their heads and their eyes stared at the floor during the entire length of the sermons. That was the pattern. You stood up to sing, then drifted off into a spiritual coma until you heard the magic words, "And so it should be with all of us …" as the minister would provide a one-sentence wrap-up of the homily. You'd stand again to sing a final hymn, hoping that the piano player was as hungry as you were and that the minister would suggest omitting verses five through eleven.

But in Ann's first sermon … they allowed each new minister one sermon before nodding off for the remainder of his pastorate … she had them. She told her life story … the story of her salvation … the story of her wayward life before coming face to face with Christ in a Nashville motel room and how she had struggled ever since to simply walk beside him. The youth of the church were amazed and fascinated by this sort of honesty in the pulpit, and Wanda and her friends began making plans to make Ann's life miserable enough that she'd receive a call from God to please go elsewhere. Her sermons were filled with questions that excited the youth, and they were devoid of the answers that would please their parents and grandparents.

Her politics didn't help her popularity. Oh, she didn't believe in preaching politics from the pulpit but her detractors were delighted to find that she would honestly answer all baited inquiries:

Abortion … "It's much bigger than a law, I'm afraid. Let's not get the government in the business of life and death. I think Christ would have me run into the arms of that hurting young mother. She needs love right now, not regulation."

The Death Penalty … "I'm afraid I'm not wise enough to determine another person's fate. Their soul is so much more important. Let's talk about that."

A woman's place in society: "I think it's so exciting that a young girl today has the world of choices open to her."

To the listener looking to find fault, Ann's answers only meant that she could not give a straight answer … one more reason a woman had no place in the Homerville pulpit.

The phone rang. It was Richard Smiley, the head of the Trustees committee.

"Are the lilies ordered?"

"Uh … I'm sorry. Who is this?"

"Sorry. This is Richard. I was wondering about the Easter lilies for the pulpit."

Richard Smiley never wondered about anything. He didn't have to. His wife Marie did all the wondering and Richard had devoted himself to a lifetime of carrying the messages from Marie to the rest of the world.

"Good morning, Richard. So good to hear your voice. How's Marie?"

"Great. Have the lilies been ordered?"

Pastor Ann had decided to do away with the annual explosion of flora on the altar this year. By the time each family had donated money for an Easter lily in memory of a departed loved one, the only thing missing was a casket. The church looked like a funeral home on Easter morning.

"You know we always have the lilies on the altar."

Grandma Doris would say, "Choose your battles, girl. Don't waste your powder on muskrats. Save it for the buffalo."

"That's on my list of things to do this afternoon, Richard. Thanks so much for calling."

"We … I … just wanted to check."

"They're on to me," thought Ann. "They read my mind and they're checking." Asthma would lose another round this Easter and the church would once again do its imitation of the Precious Moments Chapel.

Before he hung up, one final check: "The sermon coming okay?"

"Do you mean the Easter sermon?"

"Yeh. Everything coming along okay?"

Never in the course of Ann's short pastorate had anyone inquired as to her progress in sermon writing. Something was afoot. They truly did suspect her of trying to pull a fast one.

"We … I … really like the Easter story," said Richard. "Mary coming to the empty tomb then running back to tell the disciples. Just wouldn't be Easter without our traditional sermon."

This was a buffalo.

"I've been praying about the sermon all week, Richard. I think God has given me a beautiful message for this Sunday."

"The good old traditional story, eh?"

"I truly believe it's from God, so it will be beautiful. Was there anything else, Richard?"

A silence, then, "Well … just checking. See you on Sunday."

"Blessings, my friend." She hung up first.

No doubt now. The scouts had been sent out. She had nothing but admiration for the men of her Homerville congregation but she was not fool enough to believe that they did any original thinking. The waves of discontent were getting larger and more threatening and she knew their source.

If the services at the Homerville Methodist ever started late … and they usually did … it was because Pastor Ann was still making the rounds. No matter what door you entered, no matter where you sat, and even if you wanted to escape Pastor Ann's welcome, you shook her hand before the service. Not the obligatory handshake of a political candidate or a car salesman but a genuine greeting followed by as much conversation as you'd like. Ann felt that this was maybe the most important part of the service … talking, sharing, and looking deeply into the eyes of her congregation.

She knew the problem with clergy and speakers in general who come in with their own set agenda then blithely spout forth for a period of time with no idea where the congregation is living and breathing … with what they were feeling. Ann's greatest gift as a clergy was her ability to feel … her sensitivity to those around her. One of her youth group put it, "It's so cool … like she can walk into a room and in two seconds know who's hurting."

Ann privately called this "the thorn in her side." She once wrote in her prayer diary, "Feeling has a downside … you can feel everything."

As Ann would walk from person to person before each service, she'd reach down and touch a hand. If there was a handbook for Midwest hand touching, it would include something like, "Okay for grandmothers, doctors, undertakers, and paramedics. All other should keep their hands to their sides." Ann never bought into this philosophy. Both her faith and her Texas upbringing had taught her to be open with her concern. This alternately pleased and embarrassed Homerville men and it set their wives' teeth on edge. No one should be nicer to my husband than I am.

The phone.

"Pastor Ann?"

"Good morning. Who is this?"

"Would it be okay for Marcia to have her picture taken with you after the confirmation this Sunday?"

"Oh. Mrs. Lyle. Good to hear from you … and of course, I'd be delighted to …"

"She's wearing her white confirmation gown. That'll make a nice picture."

"Marcia would compliment any outfit. I'd be happy to …"

"That'll match your white robe, don't you think? Not a lot of colors … just white."

When Pastor Ann was ordained, her father gave her a white pulpit gown. He had done some researching and found the same style worn by Calvin, Huss, and other leaders of the reformation. Her mother gave her a white stole, the symbol of being yoked to Christ. Ann cherished both gifts from her parents and had no intention of wearing either. To Ann, being yoked with Christ meant not being set apart from his humanity. She preferred simple dresses or suits. And this Sunday was to be the coming-out day for the paisley rainbow of joy around her neck. This Sunday meant celebration.

"Well, I've not quite decided on what I shall wear this Sunday, but …"

"Pastor Hinley always wore his white robe thing on Easter. It was beautiful."

"I'm sure that all eyes will be on your Marcia Sunday, and it doesn't really matter what …"

"I'll have plenty of film. See you Sunday."

"Goodbye, Mrs. Lyle."

The wagons are beginning to circle. Pastor Ann looked at the shimmering rainbow of color folded neatly beside her sermon notes. It had been nearly three years since she was first appointed to the Homerville charge and still she had never discovered who put this colorful vestment outside her door. It was a pleasant diversion during the duller moments of committee meetings, letting her eyes stray around the table to guess the identity of her fellow traveler.

On the morning before Ann's sixteenth birthday, Grandma Doris took her on a picnic. Ever since Ann was able to walk, she'd run the quarter mile to her grandmother's house on weekends, they'd pack two Orange Crush sodas and four chocolate chip cookies in a paper sack and head out across Doris's west pasture. Their destination was always the same … "The Old Jabber Oak," a large tree that had fallen across Flivver Creek many years ago. Grandma Doris named it the jabber oak when she was a young girl, and she would run across the pasture and sit to jabber with the trees, the blue jays and the mockingbirds. She'd introduced Ann to the Jabber Oak on her second birthday and it had become their secret spot.

"But tomorrow's my birthday, Grandma, not today."

"This ain't a birthday present. Tomorrow you'll be sixteen and that'll be the last I see of you."

"That's silly."

"Part … but part not. Once you get the keys to your daddy's car, this old dead oak won't seem near so appealing."

"Grandma, I will never stop coming to the Jabber Tree with you."

"Whatever you say. Now sit down and let's talk a bit. I've got something to tell you before you turn sixteen and quit listening."

Ann protested a bit more but with Grandma Doris there was no use disputing anything. She was always, at least in her presence, right. She opened the bottle of Orange Crush with only her fingernail and began.

"You're a corker, Ann, but I s'pect you know that."

"I'm like you, Grandma."

"Oh, hell, I hope not. If one generation don't improve on the next then what the hell's the use of carryin' on the race? Look me in the eye, Ann."

Ann looked at her Grandmother. The first light of this Texas morning put Doris's face into an amber silhouette. Her grandmother's face had become like the Texas landscape on which she'd lived her 81 years. … the same rugged texture, the same browns and yellows, and the same temperament.

"Let's not fool ourselves. You and I ain't gonna know each other forever … at least this side of glory …"

"Grandma …"

"Just listen. I didn't catch some deadly fever, I'm just doin' and sayin' what more folks oughta do and say."

Ann smiled. "I love you Grandma."

"You'd better. Now listen … you got a couple of mean problems inside you. You're female and you're capable. Either one alone makes for a pleasurable life and folks'll admire you for either one. But havin' both … that's gonna be a problem."

"It hasn't stopped you."

"How in the hell do you know? Who knows what I might have become? But here's the part I want you to hang onto …"

Ann listened closely. Doris's language may have been colorful and sometimes painful but her words never strayed from the mark. The woman didn't have a pretentious bone in her wiry body.

"The part I want you to remember is this … It don't matter." Doris looked at Ann, seeing how much of this buckshot had hit the target. "You understand me? It just don't matter."

"Then … I mean … why are we having this talk?"

"Because you probably won't realize it don't matter unless an old wise bird like me tells you it don't matter. The thing that matters … the only thing that matters is that you and God stay just like that …" … and Doris raised her hand from the old oak to cross two of her gnarled fingers. The old lady looked down at the two stubborn digits that arthritis had prevented from ever crossing again and said, "Well damn it, you know what I mean."

"I … I think I do."

"Ain't good enough. You gotta know. You got one job in life, girl, and that's to get close to God. That's your lifelong work and that's your only real job. Everything else is just … you know … saltcedar." Grandma loved that word. Saltcedar was a Texas weed notorious for knocking out whole populations of cottonwoods and willows. She'd used other words before she'd become a Christian and the family was mightily happy to see her settle upon saltcedar. "Everything else is just saltcedar. Don't amount to a tinker's damn. There. Now you've heard the truth from the smartest gal you've ever met."

And she had. And Ann believed it.

Pastor Ann closed her eyes and sat back in her chair. She smiled as she imagined the picture on Sunday morning … no explosion of Easter lilies, no ponderous hymns, no white vestments … just a slender young woman in a plain yellow dress, adorned with the most startling silken rainbow. She didn't even have to look at her notes to recite the sermon's final paragraph. It was written plainly on her heart by a loving hand:

Some day. Some day I will worship God in a church without seventeenth-century hymns, without 18th-century architecture, and without 16th-century ritual. Some day I will take my children into the woods and see God in the dandelions, and the muskrats, and the bullfrogs, and the butterflies. Some day ... some day I will see a real, living, loving and exciting creator. He'll walk with me and he'll talk with me and he'll tell me that I am his own … And then … then he will take my hand and we'll dance. Some day ...

A knock on her office door. Rita Lovington, local florist and head of the building committee. "Pastor Ann? Sorry … didn't mean to disturb you. Working on the sermon?" Rita had been very nice to Ann during her stay in Homerville despite the fact that the new pastor had taken a family vacation in Branson last summer and failed to remind anyone to water the roses. The roses died.

"It's finished. Hello, Rita."

"I knew you'd be busy this week, so I went ahead and ordered the lilies. Any special place you want 'em this year?"

Pastor Ann blinked. This was real. She wasn't sure where she'd been a moment ago, but Rita was reality. "I …" Grandma Doris winked at her. Pastor Ann sighed. "Put them … I don't know … wherever you usually put them."

"You got it. They're gonna look so pretty with your white preacher's robe."

Ann watched Rita retreat to her van, then carefully lifted the paisley rainbow and placed it back into its box. She picked up the well-worn notes of her Easter sermon, folded them, and laid them atop the rainbow. Pastor Ann closed the box. She picked up her pen, sighed again as Wanda's venomous smile appeared on the Easter Week page of her appointment calendar, then began to write:

And very early in the morning, the first day of the week, they came unto the sepulcher at the rising of the sun. And they said among themselves, Who shall roll us away the stone from the door of the sepulcher? ...

www.creativeideas.com